NEVER LET YOU GO

ALSO BY EMMA CARLSON BERNE

Still Waters

Hard to Get

NEVER LET YOU GO

EMMA CARLSON BERNE

SIMON PULSE

NEW YORK   LONDON   TORONTO   SYDNEY   NEW DELHI

SIMON PULSE

An imprint of Simon & Schuster Children's Publishing Division

1230 Avenue of the Americas, New York, NY 10020

First Simon Pulse paperback edition December 2012

Copyright © 2012 by Emma Bernay

All rights reserved, including the right of reproduction in whole or in part in any form.

SIMON PULSE logo and colophon are registered trademarks of Simon & Schuster, Inc.

For information about special discounts for bulk purchases, please contact Simon & Schuster Special Sales at 1-866-506-1949 or business@simonandschuster.com.

The Simon & Schuster Speakers Bureau can bring authors to your live event. For more information or to book an event contact the Simon & Schuster Speakers Bureau at 1-866-248-3049 or visit our website at www.simonspeakers.com.

Designed by Karina Granda

The text of this book was set in Caslon.

Manufactured in the United States of America

2 4 6 8 10 9 7 5 3 1

The Library of Congress has cataloged this paperback edition as follows:

Berne, Emma Carlson. Never let you go / Emma Carlson Berne. p. cm.

Summary: While working on a farm during the summer, Megan falls in love with her unstable best friend's crush, with frightening consequences.

[1. Best friends—Fiction. 2. Friendship—Fiction. 3. Love—Fiction. 4. Emotional problems—Fiction. 5. Farm life—Fiction.] I. Title.

PZ7.B455139Nev 2012   [Fic]—dc23   2011039881

ISBN 978-1-4424-4017-3 (pbk)

ISBN 978-1-4424-4018-0 (eBook)

For my mom

NEVER LET YOU GO

PROLOGUE

The party had been going on for hours. Megan knew she shouldn't have anything more to drink. Already, the edges of the dark basement room had grown fuzzy, the knots of sophomores and juniors lining the walls and lounging on the floor retreating into a vodka-induced haze. Music pounded from two huge speakers, and shadowy couples ground together like contortionists, clogging the space in front of the drinks table. Megan looked down at the big plastic cup in her hand and swirled the orange liquid before tilting a little more down her throat. Vodka and orange soda. You'd think it would be nasty, but it wasn't too bad.

She stifled a burp against the back of her hand, slowly sliding down the wall until she was sitting on the cream carpet. She could feel the bass vibrating through the floor. She edged herself over a few inches to avoid a large puddle of salsa seeping into the expensive wool and carefully propped her cup against the wall. At least she wasn't standing by herself anymore. Megan glanced at the clump of juniors sitting to her right—Kelsey, Logan, Maya, all with heavy, silky long hair, the kind that always fell into place. Megan resisted the urge to smooth her own thin, wavery strands and the cowlick that always rose up into a stubborn curl in the front. She aimed a tentative smile at Logan, who stared back blankly, as if she didn't recognize Megan.

Whatever. They were all Anna's friends anyway.

Megan picked at the carpet, willing the hotness in her face to fade. Anna was in Europe with her mother. "Promise me you'll go to Mike's party," she'd insisted before she left. "He's so sad I'm abandoning him for Europe." She and Megan had been sitting on the wall outside Anna's house, eating Funyuns. Anna delicately poked her hand into the bright yellow bag. Even eating greasy onion rings, she'd still managed to look like an Irish princess. "Promise! He wants everyone to come—even you."

Even you. Megan tried to wrap her mind around the words, but the moment had passed. Just like always. "Okay," she'd said. "I will." Of course she would. She always did what Anna asked. Which was why she was here, at Anna's boyfriend's party, alone. Megan gulped the rest of her drink down in one swallow and paused, coughing a little, as the girls sitting beside her seemed to grow larger, then smaller.

Kelsey looked over. "Nice, Megan," she said, grinning and patting Megan on the back.

"Yeah, go crazy!" Maya jumped up, pumping her hips back and forth as she chanted, "Go, Megan, go, Megan, go Megan. . . ."

In a far corner of her mind, the sober corner, Megan knew

they were making fun of her, but it didn't seem so shameful right then. Just friendly and funny. She giggled and climbed to her feet as the rest of the girls started dancing in a circle, swaying and waving their arms in the air. The heavy, insistent beat of the music pounded in Megan's bones. The space grew more crowded. People pressed in from all sides and Megan gulped for air like a goldfish. Sweat trickled down the side of her neck and into her bra. Surreptitiously, Megan swiped at the front of her shirt just as Mike's bulky figure loomed in the semidarkness like a panther.

"Hey!" Logan greeted Mike with a squeal. The girls widened their circle, making a space for him, but instead Mike slipped behind Kelsey, putting his arms around her waist. They danced like that for a second before Kelsey broke away, laughing. Logan grabbed her by the hands, whispering something in her ear.

The other girls drifted into the mass of people. Not that it mattered. The music was hypnotic now, not jarring. Megan closed her eyes, extending her hands out as she danced, imagining herself as some high-cheekboned hippie chick twirling in front of a stage at Woodstock. In another level of her mind, she congratulated herself for not dancing around like an out-of-sync gerbil.

Someone touched her waist. Megan turned as a thick pair of arms slid around her middle. She looked up into Mike's face, floating above her, grinning and sweaty. "Having fun?" he shouted over the music. His hands rubbed the small of her back. Megan tried to keep a few inches between them.

"Yeah!" she shouted back. They were practically screaming. "Do you miss Anna?"

"What?" He cupped his ear.

Megan shook her head. It was probably a stupid question to ask at a party anyway. Mike pulled her closer as they danced. His belt buckle dug into the waist of her jeans.

Hang on. Megan darted a glance left and right. No one was paying attention to them. *Don't be so uptight.*

"Hey, you look really pretty," Mike shouted.

Megan glanced down at her white tank top. It had taken her an hour to decide what to wear. "Thanks!" She bit the inside of her cheek to keep from smiling idiotically.

Mike nodded along with the music and ran his hands up and down her back. *Is he coming on to me? Mike? Anna's boyfriend. What is he doing?* His hips ground against hers. *Definitely coming on to me.* He was holding her really close now. She could see the blond stubble on his chin. She'd never danced like this with a guy, not with a big, sexy guy like Mike. It was beyond nice. Actually, it was so beyond nice that Megan could barely keep a coherent thought in her head.

Megan could feel people looking at them now. They were watching her grind with her best friend's boyfriend. Megan knew that with certainty. This was wrong in every sense and she couldn't care less, much less stop herself, because Mike's breath was on her face, and every fiber of her body, which had completely divorced itself from her mind, was reaching up toward him as he leaned down.

Then it was happening. It really was. Mike was kissing her. His tongue was in her mouth. Her legs were shaking. She felt like hot oil was running over every inch of her skin.

You are kissing Mike! her mind screamed, but her stubborn, rebellious body refused to listen. It just kissed him back with her arms locked around his neck.

Then his grip changed. Mike's hands weren't around her waist anymore, they were around her neck, wrapped around her throat. His thumbs pressed insistently on her windpipe even as he kept kissing her. Megan wrenched her head back and her eyelids flew open like a startled sparrow's as she choked, but he would not let go. *Why is the room so dark?* Her lungs were tight, screaming for air as he squeezed harder. *Why is his face so blurry?* It didn't even look like Mike—his features looked smaller, softer. It wasn't Mike at all, it was Anna. And Anna's hands were around her neck, squeezing harder and harder as Megan gasped for air, Anna's berry-painted lips stretching in a wide grin because she'd found out, she knew what Megan had done. . . .

CHAPTER 1

The bus bumped over a pothole and Megan woke with a start, jerking her head from the hot pane of glass where it had been resting. She eased the twisted strap of her canvas bag from across her body. It took her a minute to get it off, then she laid her head back against the blue plastic seat. Her heart was hammering like a scared rabbit's. *What a dream.* She sat still, trying to recover, staring at the metal ceiling of the bus, where a red and white square was marked IN EMERGENCY, PULL HANDLE, THEN PUSH DOOR OUTWARD. Megan briefly pictured herself standing on the seat, pushing the hatch open. It would be cooler with the wind whipping past.

Mike. God, why was she thinking about *that* debacle? It was over, finished, done with last summer. Megan reached into her khaki messenger bag and pulled out a stainless-steel water bottle. She took a long drink, grimacing at the warm, flat taste. *Don't play dumb*, she told herself. She knew why she was thinking about that night—it was exactly one year ago today. One year ago that she made the biggest mistake of her life. And almost lost her best friend forever. Almost.

To distract herself, Megan focused on the back of the bus driver—straight coffee-colored neck, neat blue polyester collar. The other bus riders seemed practically comatose, beaten into submission by the stench of the clogged lavatory at the back. To Megan's right, a young blond woman cradled a sleeping toddler, the child's head flung back. A girl about Megan's own age sat in front of them, slumped down. Behind Megan, someone was snoring rhythmically, with a sound like a small chainsaw.

The sun beat through the windows, filling the coach with the smell of hot gym shoes, despite the best efforts of the asthmatic air conditioner, which whistled through the vents over their heads. It had been four hours of corn and soybeans under the whitish sky, broken by the occasional truck-stop exit full of belching semis and minivans stuffed with sticky children. But at least Anna was waiting for her at the other end.

Megan dug out her phone and thumbed through Anna's last e-mail, sent yesterday.

> Pick you up in front of the restaurant on the main street. I think it's called the Leaf. The farm looks gorgeous—I can't believe it's been three years since I was last up here. You are going to love it. I'm so excited we get to work together!!!

Megan stared out the window. The landscape was starting to get more hilly now, with patches of lush woods flashing past. When Anna asked Megan to work with her at her uncle Thomas's farm this summer, Megan had been so excited. Anna used to go down there every summer, back before her dad left. Then, a few months ago, her uncle called and said that her aunt had started using a wheelchair because of her MS and he needed some extra help. Anna had arrived last week to get started.

Megan gazed apprehensively out the window at a giant green tractor trawling slowly up and down a sea of waving corn leaves. No—it wasn't going to be like that. She scrolled through the e-mail again. "—*ten pigs, chickens, a big garden, and horses!*" Anna had written. That didn't sound too bad. More like the Richard Scarry books she used to read when she was little. She scanned the rest of the e-mail.

> And we get a separate place to sleep too, just
> for the two of us. Oh, yeah. There's a surprise
> too. I won't say too much now, but it's definitely
> going to make this summer way more fun.

The bus swayed as the driver guided it around a hairpin turn. They were going into some sort of valley now, with trees crowding right up against the road. Megan caught a glimpse of a rushing creek, more like a little river. She wondered what the surprise was. Anna's surprises could be odd sometimes. Like the time she'd made T-shirts for Megan and her with Mr. O'Gorman's picture on it. He was their eighth-grade history teacher, and they both had crushes on him at the time. Anna thought they should wear the shirts to school. Megan had told her that would be way too embarrassing, which Anna didn't understand at all. She'd said it would be funny. Megan had refused and Anna shredded both shirts with her mother's meat scissors.

The bus reached the bottom of the valley. Black cows stood with their heads buried in knee-high grass, their tails switching. The other bus riders were waking up, gathering their possessions. The snorer behind her sat up with a grunt and belched. Megan craned her neck to look through the windshield. She could see nothing but the tops of some buildings partially hidden by a low hill. That must be the town, Ault Flats. Megan felt a wriggle of anticipation in her belly.

The driver rolled through a stop sign, made a sharp left, then braked abruptly. He cut the engine and opened the door with a pneumatic hiss. It seemed very quiet without the engine noise. Megan watched the other riders file down the aisle. She hitched her messenger bag over her shoulder and wrestled her duffel down from the metal rack overhead. This was it. She was here.

As Megan climbed down the steep black steps, the heat hit her like a furnace blast. It radiated up through the soles of her sandals and pressed against her face. Megan found herself alone on a cracked sidewalk.

Buildings lined either side of the short street—the only road in the town, as far as Megan could tell. There was a worn-out pharmacy, a pawn shop, a barnlike structure with bags of fertilizer stacked out front and a sign reading BAKER'S FEED AND SEED, a repair shop with a disemboweled tractor visible in the open bay, and a liquor store.

Her palms were sweaty and her messenger bag was cutting into her shoulder. Megan changed her grip on her duffel, scanning the buildings for the Leaf. The sun was a pale disk burning through the dull clouds. It was so quiet, Megan's sandals scraped on the gritty sidewalk as she turned around. This place was really remote. She'd kind of been picturing something . . . cuter. And Anna wasn't here. Megan tried to tamp down her annoyance. Maybe the bus had been early. She glanced at her phone. No. Right on time.

A few men with weather-seamed faces sat outside the repair shop, perched on metal barrels. Megan felt their eyes on her legs and she swallowed, trying not to feel self-conscious. She wished she'd worn jeans instead of shorts. Where the hell was the damn Leaf restaurant? Did Anna have the name wrong or— She spotted a green and white sign across the street with a surge of relief and marched purposefully toward it.

Megan set her bags down between her feet and leaned awkwardly against a windowsill, folding her arms on her chest and trying to look nonchalant. *Don't those gross old guys have anything else to do? Fix some tractors or something?* One with a bushy brown beard winked at her. Megan gritted her teeth and looked steadily and deliberately at the yellow shop sign next door. J&B PAWN, SINCE 1960.

Just then, she heard the rumble of an engine and saw a rust-red pickup roaring toward her, Anna at the wheel. Megan picked up her bags, a grin already on her face. She stepped to the curb in readiness, waving wildly as the pickup drew near. But Anna didn't stop. The truck roared past. Megan could see Anna turn her head, laughing. She disappeared down the street. Megan's hand wilted by her side, and a familiar mixture of frustration and resignation rose in her throat. She stood, her face flaming as the men in front of the repair shop chortled. At the end of the street, the truck screeched in a U-turn and drove back toward her. This time, Anna stopped and Megan ran to the passenger door, wrenching it open in a shower of rust flakes.

"Hey!" Anna said, still laughing. "Got you! Your face when I drove past was hilarious." Her sunglasses covered half her cheeks, like she had huge fly eyes. Her glossy black hair was twisted on top of her head, and she wore a clingy gray T-shirt and jeans cut off just above her knees.

Megan tucked her messenger bag behind her feet and flung her duffel in the back. It was just Anna being Anna. "Those old guys at the garage thought it was hilarious too." Megan kept her voice light.

"You look gorgeous, by the way." Anna reached over and gave Megan a one-armed hug as she drove. "I'm so glad to see you!"

"You too," Megan replied and suddenly, she was. Anna's presence was like a firework—sizzling, bright, colorful. She relaxed back against the seat, which was covered with an old gray blanket, sprinkled liberally with dog hair. She cranked the window down as far as it would go and let the breeze dry her sweat-dampened hair. "This truck is great. Really . . . farm-y."

"Yeah, Uncle Thomas let me borrow it to come get you. And it's a stick shift! Can you believe I'm driving it?"

"No, not really." Megan watched her friend's sneakered feet alternately press the pedals on the floor. "Do I have to drive it?"

"Probably. We use it all the time for hay and feed and stuff." Anna shifted expertly into third gear.

"Oh." A few shreds of straw blew up from the floor of the cab and whirled around her knees. "How's it been so far? It feels like you left way longer than a week ago."

Anna nodded. "I know. *So* much has happened too," she bubbled. Megan was about to ask what she meant, but Anna kept talking. "How was home?"

Megan made a face. "Boring. Mom made me take online tours of colleges with her all week."

Anna slowed down behind a trailer full of cows. "Ick. Why didn't you just tell her to stop?"

"Oh, sure. She'd love that. Then you'd be working down here by yourself this summer because I'd be confined to the house." Megan extracted her water bottle again and took a drink. "So, what's it *like*, you know, working on a farm? I'm kind of nervous." For an instant, she wished she could take the words back before Anna gave her that look like she was the most idiotic person in the world. But her friend just reached out and squeezed her knee.

"It's fun. You'll love it, I promise. Uncle Thomas does all the serious plowing and mowing and stuff. The summer hands mostly do the garden and the chores."

"Chores?" It sounded like a Laura Ingalls Wilder story. They were always doing chores in those books.

"Like feeding the animals and mucking and gathering eggs. And you're getting paid! It's better than Silver Mountain."

They looked at each other and Megan snorted, then they burst out laughing. They'd both applied to work at the Silver Mountain jewelry kiosk in the mall before Thomas had called. The woman who ran the place looked like she ate high schoolers for snacks.

Megan offered the water to Anna. "Is it weird seeing your aunt in a wheelchair?" she asked sympathetically.

"No." Anna's voice was hard. She took a long swig.

Megan raised her eyebrows. "It was just a question." More fences, more cows outside. Clapboard farmhouses with American flags. Children's toys in the driveways. A field of sheep that looked like dingy cotton balls with legs.

Anna sighed, capped the bottle with one hand, and handed it back. "Aunt Linda and I don't really get along, okay? She's never liked me, because I've always been Uncle Thomas's favorite. She's jealous." Anna's fingers tightened on the steering wheel.

"Oh." Megan searched her mind for a new subject. Making Anna mad was never a good idea. She glanced at her friend's toned arms. "How is it that you already have a tan?"

Anna's face lightened, and she laughed as if she knew how great she looked. "Ten hours in the sun every day? I've mostly been working in the garden this week." The corners of her lips turned up and she lingered over the words, as if drawing up pleasant memories.

"By yourself?"

"No . . . Uncle Thomas has some full-time help. Dave and Sarah. They're, like, twenty-five."

The road was straight now, and the cows had given way to open fields of some kind of low, curly plant. Anna pressed her foot on the accelerator. She gave Megan a significant look.

"Okay, I give in," Megan said. "Come on, what's the surprise? I know you're dying to tell me."

Anna seemed to hold herself in for a moment, then burst out, "Oh my God, Megan, I *met* someone and he's so perfect! I was going to wait and not say anything until later, but I just *have* to tell you. His name is Jordan and he's one of the other summer hands. He started the same time as me, and he's so sweet. We've been hanging out all week and it's getting really serious. I think that he could be, you know, *the one*." She was practically bouncing in her seat, her eyes hot and bright.

Megan could feel sweat break out on her upper lip, despite the breeze from the open window. "Oh, wow!" she said, trying for simple excitement. Anna hadn't gone out with anyone since she and Mike had broken up. No one ever said it was because of what happened at the party, but by the time school started in the fall, Anna and Mike were over. During the initial explosion, Megan had sobbed and apologized. Anna called every single night to tell Megan just how furious she was. Then, after one month exactly, Anna never spoke of it again. She would completely shut down when Megan attempted to broach the subject.

Anna watched her, glancing frequently at the road. Megan licked her lips. "That is so great." She felt like she was balancing on a slick stepping stone in the middle of a creek. One misstep and she'd fall in. "I'm really happy for you." If Anna could find someone new, maybe the wound would be healed. The wound Megan had created. A fresh wave of guilt swamped her, somehow undiminished despite the passage of twelve months.

Megan reached over and grasped Anna's hand for a second. "I am so happy for you," she repeated, looking right at her friend. *Please, Anna. Believe me. Should I say something more? Like an anniversary apology?*

"Thanks." Anna squeezed Megan's hand and then released it to turn onto a narrower side road. "I'm happy for me too."

The weeks of the summer stretched out like a long, murky river. They would be together every day, sleeping together, eating together. Megan had to get it out in the open. She had to say something about the anniversary. *Okay. Say it now. "I just wanted to tell you how sorry . . . You know, today is one year . . . I'm so glad we're still friends after . . ."* But the passage of time weighed on Megan, and instead she let out her breath and rested her head against the scratchy blanket. They were quiet for a few miles. The breeze blowing through the window was cooler now, almost refreshing. Trees were everywhere, huge towering oaks and maples with long grass laid over in swaths around their trunks. They passed an old red brick house, like something out of *Pride and Prejudice*, then a mowed pasture with horse jumps. The next house was a massive Tudor concoction surrounded by landscaped grounds. Megan blinked. "I'm sorry, are we in another state? Why does everything look like it's from a Jane Austen novel all of a sudden?"

Anna laughed. "I know, weird, isn't it? It's all farms and cows, and then it turns into this super-fancy area called Ault Hill." They passed a twenty-five miles per hour sign, and Anna slowed, downshifting. "It's all big estates. A lot of people just come out here on the weekends to ride their horses." She gestured at a cream-colored barn that looked bigger than their high school at home. "Uncle Thomas has one of the only working farms in this section. He says the county association is always calling, asking if he wants to sell, so they can break it up into estates."

Anna flicked on the turn signal and braked rapidly. Megan saw a stone pillar with a plaque set into it reading GIVEN FARM. In front of them stretched a long gravel driveway, flanked by open pastures, which disappeared into trees up ahead.

"This is it," Anna said, turning into the drive. "Welcome home."

CHAPTER 2

Gravel sprayed from beneath the truck tires as they pulled to the side of a neat, white, wood-frame house. Anna opened the door and jumped down from the truck. Megan followed more slowly with her heavy duffel.

She glimpsed a large red barn to the left, and a few other out-buildings beyond. The front door of the house was open, and on the steps several pairs of rubber boots were lined up by size. The lawn was neatly mowed, and a long picnic table sat prominently under two huge oak trees.

A piece of gravel worked its way into Megan's open sandal, and she shook her foot, wishing for the sneakers in her bag. She looked up to see two men, one older, one young, coming out of the barn with a huge black cowlike animal in between them. They each held a long rope attached to either side of the cow's halter. A pretty girl in her twenties with braids halfway down her back walked to the side, holding a long blue wand.

"Easy, easy!" the older man said. He had a ruddy face and a shock of white hair. The beast snorted and whipped its head back and forth like he was trying to stampede down the driveway.

Anna grabbed Megan's arm and pulled her back a little. "That's Samson!" she whispered excitedly. "They're taking him to the pasture across the road."

"What is it?" Megan murmured back. She didn't know why they were whispering, but the whole situation seemed very tense and maybe Samson didn't like loud noises.

Anna looked at her like she was missing half her brain. "A bull, Megan!"

"Ohh," Megan breathed, taking another look at Samson. She could see it perfectly now. He looked just like Ferdinand.

"None of the fences on this side of the farm are strong enough to keep him contained," a voice said from behind them.

Megan turned. A middle-aged woman with a gray pixie cut was maneuvering an electric wheelchair out through the porch door.

"Samson is a lovely bull, but he's getting a little cheeky for his own good. Burst through two gates last week. Dave built him a new pen across the road." The woman had a wide, pleasant face and a matter-of-fact way of speaking.

Samson was getting closer now. Megan could hear him snorting wetly and grunting low in his chest as he and his handlers approached.

The men didn't speak or acknowledge the girls. Megan wasn't sure they'd even seen them, since they were so focused on the bull, but the girl with the braids looked up and nodded briefly. Just then, Samson gave an especially violent tug at his ropes, and the two men—Megan figured the older one must be Thomas— hung on tightly, sweat visible on their foreheads.

Megan backed up a little farther until she stumbled against the porch steps. She grabbed at the railing to keep from falling.

"That's right, better come up here, girls," Linda said. "He gets agitated so easily."

Megan scurried up the three steps, but Anna leaned against the truck, one foot flat against the door, knee bent, as she picked idly at a scrape on her knee.

"Anna, come up here." Linda spoke more sharply.

Anna still didn't move.

"Anna!" Megan hissed.

Anna rolled her eyes. "Calm down, Megan. You've only been here five minutes and you're already freaking out."

Megan flinched at Anna's words and glanced quickly at Linda, wondering if she agreed. But Linda was still frowning at Anna.

Samson passed the truck, his hooves crunching on the gravel, and headed slowly down the long driveway toward the road.

Megan let out a breath she didn't realize she'd been holding. Her first interaction with a bull—well, sort of—and she hadn't been trampled. Things were starting off well.

Linda buzzed her wheelchair over a few feet. "I'm Linda, by the way. You must be Megan. We're so glad you could help us out this summer."

"Oh, me too. I've never been on a farm before, though—I hope that's okay." Megan smiled sheepishly, but the older woman looked unperturbed.

"You'll catch on fast, I'm sure. Anna will show you every-thing you need to know. She's practically an expert!" Linda raised her voice in enthusiasm, but the words rang hollowly. Anna just stared off toward the barn.

Megan's cheeks flushed with embarrassment at her friend's rudeness. Megan focused on the end of the driveway, where a figure had appeared, walking toward them, alone. The girl with braids panted up a few minutes later, still holding her stick. She was wearing a man's button-up shirt untucked with the sleeves rolled up and a pair of paint-splattered khaki shorts.

"Whew!" She dropped onto the porch step next to Megan and wiped her dripping forehead with the hem of her shirt. "Well, I'm glad that's done for the summer."

"Did they get him in?" Linda asked with a touch of anxiety.

"Yeah. Dave's reinforcing the gate right now." She turned to Megan. "I'm Sarah. The other guy with Samson was Dave, my boyfriend. We help out Thomas and Linda on the farm. He's heavy machinery, I'm cooking and housekeeping."

"And honorary daughter." Linda patted Sarah's shoulder. Anna was still pointedly ignoring the conversation.

"Hi. I'm Megan," Megan said, waving a little. *That probably looked stupid*, she chastised herself, but Sarah just nodded.

"Want a muffin? I made them this morning—green apple." She was already halfway into the house.

"I'm okay. Um, what's that?" Megan pointed at the stick now lying on the porch. It was about three feet long and had a small fork at one end, kind of like a blue devil's pitchfork.

Sarah stopped and looked back. "That's an electric goad. To shock the panties off Samson in case he feels like misbehaving."

Linda turned her wheelchair around, and Sarah held the door open for her. "Thomas will show you around when he gets back, Megan," Linda said over her shoulder. "He likes to do a tour whenever we have new help." The screen door slapped behind them.

"*Bzzz,*" Anna said, finally joining Megan on the porch. "I touched one once when I was little. For a minute, I thought I was dead."

Megan eyed Anna, trying to figure out if she was still pissy about Linda. But her friend just picked up the electric goad and flipped it around in her hand.

"I remember that. I had to pick you up off the barn floor," a voice said behind them. Megan turned to see Thomas, minus Samson. Dave stood beside him, holding a hammer in one dirt-stained hand.

"Uncle Thomas! I'm glad Samson didn't gore you!" Anna flung herself off the porch and wrapped her arms around the older man's waist. Megan blinked in surprise. That greeting seemed a little over the top.

Thomas must have thought so too, because he patted Anna's back and gently extricated himself. "Now, now. He doesn't have any horns, doll."

"Oh, yeah. I forgot." She offered her uncle a charming smile. Thomas lifted his eyebrows toward Megan.

"Oops, sorry. This is Megan," Anna said, gesturing as if Megan was a kid tagging along for the day.

Megan shook his hand, which was so rough and hard, it felt like rhino skin. His fingernails were cut short and rimmed with dirt. "Glad you made it down here, Megan."

Dave broke in. "If you need me, I'll be harrowing the oats." He had a bushy black beard and black eyes that were hooded but alert.

"Be sure to get the northwest corner," Thomas told him. "Big stand of skunkweed Jordan's back there."

Anna drew in her breath sharply, then poked Megan in the side.

Dave nodded and waved to the girls as he left.

"Let me show you around, Megan." Thomas led the way past the house, where the gravel drive cut through the farm itself, dividing it in half. He walked with a long, effortless stride, and Megan had to quicken her pace to keep up. Her feet slid in the gravel, and she wished to God she'd worn anything except sandals. She glanced longingly at Anna's sturdy sneakers and Thomas's heavy rubber boots. Thomas was going to think she was some kind of silly city girl. She hoped they wouldn't meet anyone else until she could change her shoes.

Beside her, Anna swung her arms energetically as they walked. "Isn't this place gorgeous?" she chattered. "I seriously think this is, like, my favorite place on earth. After Dad left—"

"Here are the horses," Thomas interrupted smoothly. They approached the red barn. Its cream trim was neatly painted, and there was a fenced pasture to the left. A mud puddle stretched in front of the open double doors. Megan eyed it cautiously, tiptoeing around the edge as Thomas splashed straight through.

The barn was vast inside, with empty stalls stretching down each side and the ceiling soaring at least fifty feet overhead. A crammed hayloft stretched high along one wall, but the barn floor was neatly swept.

Two huge brown horses poked their heads out of their stall doors as the three walked down the aisle. "Awww," Megan couldn't help breathing. They had massive heads and necks and thick blond forelocks. Beside them, a gray donkey bobbed his head up and down in greeting.

She'd never outgrown her little-girl love for horses, though she hadn't been near one for years. Even now she wished it wasn't babyish to have horse pictures in her room the way she used to when she was younger. Those glossy ones with the horses running across mountain meadow or grazing in fields of buttercups.

Anna patted the donkey's head briskly. "Hi, Cisco."

"These are Belgian draft horses," Thomas told Megan. "Rosie's on the right and Darryl's on the left. I've decided to try horse-drawn plowing this year, as an experiment, so they arrived in the spring." He stepped up and rubbed his hand under Rosie's heavy blond mane. "Rosie here came in foal. She's going to be having a baby very, very soon." He pointed, and Megan noticed the mare's bulging sides.

"Oooh," she breathed, enchanted. "When is she going to have her baby? Is Darryl the father?" Tentatively, Megan patted the mare's warm nose, which was pricked with a few stiff whiskers.

Anna laughed and twisted around from where she was sitting on a nearby bale of hay. "No, dork. Darryl's a gelding." Darryl snuffled as if agreeing.

Megan flushed and glanced hesitantly at Thomas.

"A castrated male horse," he supplied. "No, the father's on the other farm. And she's due sometime this week, I think." He walked back toward the door. "The summer hands trade off stall cleaning, and feeding and watering twice daily. The horses get turned out onto that grass." He pointed to the opposite door, which led directly out to the fenced pasture.

Then Thomas led them out of the barn and past an open shed where a large tractor and several small tractors were parked. A dizzying array of pitchforks, rakes, shovels, hoes, and wheelbarrows were against one wall, while another was lined with labeled metal trash cans.

"Machine shed," Thomas said. "This is also where we keep most of the animal feed. Shavings for bedding are in a shed behind the barn, and the manure pile is beyond the horse pasture."

Megan's temples were beginning to feel tight with all the information. She nodded, trying to look capable and enthusiastic. Manure pile. That's something she wouldn't have encountered working at the mall.

Thomas must have noticed her worried expression. "I know it seems like a lot now, but you'll be amazed at how fast you'll get into the routine. Anna only comes up in the summer, but the minute she's here, it's like she never left." He looked affectionately at Anna, who pursed her lips in an "aw shucks" way.

Megan could tell she was eating up the praise. She looked away, tasting a familiar feeling of sadness and irritation. Anna could act so *needy* around men. Needy and puppyish. She was always like this at home, with their other friends' fathers and the track coach and the teachers at school. *God, do you have to have constant attention?* Megan always wanted to shout at her. *Can someone* not *admire you for one second?*

About fifty feet ahead, a large wire pen held ten pigs, all stretched out in the dirt, eyes tightly closed.

"Naptime," Thomas said.

The smell was intense. Megan resisted the urge to pull the collar of her shirt up over her nose. Anna didn't seem to notice, though, as she leaned on the fence.

"They get kind of aggressive at feeding time," she said cheerfully. "You just have to be careful they don't knock you down. You'll get trampled."

Megan cleared her throat and leaned against the fence beside Anna. "Right. I can handle that." She *sounded* confident at least. *Please, don't let me do anything stupid this summer.* She didn't want to spend the next ten weeks slipping in the mud and getting trampled by hungry pigs.

Thomas continued up the drive. "Come on, girls. We'll go up to the fields and the sheep pasture."

Anna rushed to her uncle's side. Megan wondered at her

hurry until she remembered that the mysterious Jordan was in the fields. Hurrying to catch up, Megan turned from the pigs, but her sandal caught on a piece of wire sticking out from the fence, causing her foot to slip out. She stumbled and brought her bare foot down in a mucky puddle. "Shit!" Megan whispered to herself as she tried to scrape the mud off on the edge of the fence. Great. She stuck her foot back in her sandal anyway, then hurried after Anna and Thomas, who were now far ahead.

"What happened to your foot?" Anna asked loudly the minute Megan caught up to them.

"Nothing, I just stepped in a little mud." She could tell Anna knew exactly what had happened, but pointing out Megan's blunders was one of her favorite activities. It was a kind of hobby, like stamp collecting. This time, though, Anna didn't say anything more.

They were approaching a large field of tall plants. Megan figured that must be oats, since it didn't look like hay or corn. She could just make out someone on a tractor in the far corner. There was another person lifting something on the ground nearby.

Anna grabbed Megan's upper arm and squeezed painfully. "That's him!" she hissed.

Megan squinted. "He looks like a dot," she murmured back.

"But a really cute dot, right?" Anna gazed adoringly into the distance.

Thomas glanced at his watch. "You won't have to do much with these crops, but oats, hay, and corn are in these three fields." He strode over the long grass, navigating the big matted clumps skillfully. "But sheep are in this far pasture." He gestured to a flock nibbling grass. A long, open shelter was built into one corner of the pasture.

"Here, Megan, hose your foot off in the pump." Thomas stopped and indicated an old-fashioned hand pump on a pad of concrete nearby. While Megan washed, he went on. "You all will come up here every day to check their water and throw hay." He turned around and fixed the girls with a stern but not unkind look. "It's important that these chores get done well and get done on time."

"Uncle Thomas," Anna pouted. "Don't lecture us. . . ." She smiled at him winsomely. "We *know*."

"Well, it's the obligatory mean-boss talk." He waggled his eyebrows at them, and the girls followed him along the fence line.

Megan struggled along in the long grass, the sharp blades scraping her calves. *How big is this place?* It felt like they'd been walking for miles. The sun blazed down, sending up the nutty scent of toasting seeds.

To Megan's surprise, there were several more buildings laid out in front of them: a barn silvery gray with age with a partially caved-in roof and some smaller sheds that leaned precariously, with most of the glass in the windows broken or missing. A rail fence around the perimeter was mostly knocked over.

"This is the old section of the farm," Thomas said, gazing at the abandoned structures with his hands on his hips. "Megan, Anna already knows this, but when I bought this place back in the seventies, it was a much larger conventional farm. When I decided to go organic, I just couldn't keep up with all the maintenance. So this part is abandoned. At some point, we'll knock all this down, but for now, I don't want anyone back here. These old buildings are dangerous."

"Yes, all right." Megan wondered if she should be calling him "sir." He reminded her of the supervisor at the food bank where she used to volunteer: serious in a "don't mess with me" way, but not mean. She liked that—it seemed right for a boss.

Anna sighed. "I think it's lovely back here. So quiet and peaceful."

Thomas fixed her with a stern look. "Stay away. I mean it."

"I know, I know," Anna conceded, which seemed to satisfy him.

They turned down a little dirt footpath carved into an open field back toward the farmhouse. Thomas stopped, and Megan almost ran into his back. To their left, a little wooden cabin with a sloping tin roof and a minuscule front porch stood as if it had sprouted directly out of the field. Megan half expected to see one of the Seven Dwarfs step through the door.

Anna grabbed Megan's hand. "This is our place!" She ran Megan up to the porch, swinging her hand.

"You settle in, Megan," Thomas called. "I'll drop off your bags in a few minutes. We didn't get to the chickens or the garden, but Anna can show you those later. Our welcome dinner will be at six at the farmhouse."

"Thanks, Uncle Thomas!" Anna called over her shoulder.

"Yeah, thanks," Megan echoed.

Thomas waved and continued down on the footpath. Anna opened the screen door, and Megan followed her inside. There was only one room, just big enough for two metal cots and a trunk at the base of each bed. A rough table between the beds held a battery-powered lamp and a large can of bug spray. Red flowered curtains hung over the two tiny screened windows.

"Isn't this great?" Anna shoved an assortment of clothes off her bed and flopped onto the mattress. "Our very own place!" She smiled at Megan.

Megan grinned back, feeling the first rush of happy excitement since getting out of the truck. She suddenly remembered third grade, when she and Anna finally managed to convince their mothers to let them walk the twenty minutes to school instead of taking the bus. That first morning, Anna had pulled a white bag out of her backpack, her face wearing the same secret smile she had now. Inside the bag were Sour Patch Kids. *Candy! In the morning!* Megan remembered thinking. No one but Anna could have dared such a thing.

"—we're all by ourselves out here," Anna was saying.

"Oooh," Megan said in mock fear. "Where's everyone else sleep?" Metal springs squeaked as she perched on the other bed, which was covered with a rough wool blanket slightly damp to the touch.

"Uncle Thomas, Aunt Linda, Dave, and Sarah are all in the farmhouse, and the boys are in a bunkhouse by the horse barn. The bunkhouse was an old goat pen, but Uncle Thomas converted it for the summers. There's two other hands starting today besides you. One's Robert, and I can't remember the other's name." Anna stuffed a blue-striped pillow beneath her neck.

Megan looked around. "Uh, is there a bathroom?" She hoped this wasn't a peeing-outside kind of place. That had never been one of her talents, though Anna had always been pretty good at it whenever they went camping as kids.

"In the farmhouse. Farmhands' bathroom is off the kitchen. But look!" She rose to her knees and pointed out one of the tiny windows. Megan knelt beside her and craned her neck to look down. A troughlike metal sink was attached to the outside of the cabin. She could make out a bar of soap on a string, and a towel and mirror hanging from nails. "Isn't that cute?"

"Yeah," Megan said hesitantly as Anna lay back on the pillow again. Her friend picked up a magazine from the nightstand and flipped through it idly. Silence descended on the cabin. Outside there was a muffled *thump* as Thomas or someone dropped her bags onto the porch, then the crunch of receding footsteps. Megan could hear cicadas buzzing in the trees far away. Okay, they were finally alone. She felt like she *had* to say something about the anniversary. What if Anna was thinking about it too and waiting for her to acknowledge it somehow?

Do it. "Listen, there's something I want to tell you." A little flutter of fear brushed Megan's throat as she spoke. She remembered Anna's face crumpling with rage when she admitted that the rumors were true. The avid faces at school afterward—like hyenas circling a wounded deer, delighted at a fresh scandal. She would catch little snippets of whispered conversation when she passed in the halls. ". . . *all over* him . . . totally grinding . . . he said she's . . ." No one would talk to her—until Anna came over one day at lunch and sat down beside her. Megan knew the whole cafeteria was watching them. Anna just unzipped her lunch tote and pulled out a yogurt. Between bites, she asked Megan about the trig quiz. Megan remembered wanting to weep with shaky, grateful thankfulness.

You owe her, Megan. You still owe her.

"I had the freakiest dream on the bus," she began haltingly. "It reminded me that today is . . . one year since the Mike thing." She choked on the last sentence.

Anna's face was impassive. She didn't move or speak, just stared up at the ceiling, her hands at her sides. Megan went on, faster now, the words tumbling over each other in her hurry to get them out. "We haven't really talked about it—which is fine, totally fine—but I, um, I really want you to know that I'm so, so sorry. Again. I mean, still. I'm still sorry." She made herself stop and waited for a response.

Anna lay still for what seemed like a long time. Megan had just opened her mouth to ask if she was okay, when Anna sat upright.

"You know what? It's okay. It's all in the past." Anna's voice was bright. A spot of color burned high on each cheekbone. "What's now is now and what's past is past, right?"

"Right!" Megan tried to match Anna's chipper tone. She knew she should feel relieved, but something about her friend's voice didn't sound right. It was very happy, hyper, and each word was clipped at the end. "I just felt like I should say something—"

Anna swung her legs off the bed and stood up. "Besides"—she

threw back the lid of her trunk—"I think something might happen with Jordan tonight. He's only seen me all dirty from working. The welcome dinner is the perfect time to show him who I *really* am." She held up a strappy white sundress, then glanced over at Megan. "What are you going to wear?"

"Oh! Um, I'm not sure. I should probably unpack." She moved toward the door. *All right, that's done. And Anna said it was okay. So be happy!* But she still felt unsettled, as if the air in the cabin was vaguely toxic. *Stop! What more do you want? You said you're sorry, she said it was okay.* Megan pushed open the screechy screen door and dragged her bags inside. Then she realized why Anna's voice had bothered her. It was the same tone Anna used when they had talked about their crush on Mr. O'Gorman.

Megan dumped the contents of her tote onto the bed and started stacking clothes in the trunk, which smelled like old newspapers. She knew she should feel relieved. She *did* feel relieved. She'd apologized and it was summer and she was going to spend the whole time outside with her best friend. With a sudden lightening of the heart, Megan turned to Anna, then stopped. Her friend was kneeling on the floor, slicing away the lining of her white sundress with what looked like a straight razor, the kind that folded into a handle.

"What are you doing? Why are you cutting up your dress?"

Anna held up the shorn dress triumphantly. The shredded lining lay in a puddle on the floor. "There. It'll look way better without it." She stood up, yanked off her T-shirt, and pulled on the dress, pushing her cutoffs down around her ankles. She stepped out of them, asking, "Doesn't it? What do you think?" Anna twirled around once, letting the skirt float up around her.

The dress hung airily to midthigh, but even in the dimness of the cabin, Megan could see her lacy blue bra and bikini underwear as clearly as if Anna had been wearing plastic wrap. "Well . . . it's a bit see-through."

"Are you being uptight again?" Anna asked silkily.

Megan bit her lip.

Anna smoothed the dress against her body. "You know, Megan, I could have invited anyone up here. Maya, Logan—any of those girls. But I invited you." She looked at Megan to make sure her words had sunk in.

"I know," Megan whispered. She looked down at the blanket.

Anna smiled with satisfaction and spun around again. Something on the floor clanked by her foot. It was the razor. Megan picked it up gingerly. The blade was very shiny. "Why do you have this?"

"I read something that said you get a way closer shave with an old-fashioned razor than with those safety ones." Anna smiled beatifically. "So are you going to wear an old lady skirt, like always?"

"No," Megan said defensively. "I brought a dress too."

Anna came over and rested her head briefly on Megan's shoulder. "Sorry." She patted Megan's hair. "I'll bet whatever you brought is awesome."

Megan pulled away and laid her pink flowered dress out on the bed. It did look like an old lady dress. Why hadn't she noticed that before? She pulled it on and gazed down at the folds of soft fabric that hung to her knees. Thomas and Linda would think it was appropriate at least.

Anna leaned over a tiny mirror propped up on the bedside table, applying eyeliner in a thick black stripe, humming to herself.

Megan watched her. Maybe she should let her go out in that dress, to get back at her for the old lady crack. But no. She couldn't. Wasn't this what she and Anna always did? Protected each other. Megan protected Anna from Anna's own crazy behavior, as much as she could, and Anna protected Megan from . . . social isolation? Megan shuddered inside when she thought about where she would be without Anna. She would be like . . . well, Megan remembered an unfortunate girl in middle school who would do things like wear a ponytail smack on the top of her head. Francie would fly into rages in the hallway when she couldn't open her locker, always had body odor, and always had food on the front of her shirt. That would have been her, Megan was fairly sure.

Megan cleared her throat. "You know, that dress really *is* see-through," she tried again. "Maybe you can't tell in here, but it's like a nightgown." She tried to sound firm but gentle. "Seriously, you should wear something else." She went over to Anna's side and riffled through the jumble of clothes on the floor. "Here, how about this?" She picked up a black cotton shift. "It's totally cute."

Anna popped open a lipstick tube and painted her mouth in burgundy. She smacked her lips together, studying the effect in the mirror, then looked up at Megan. "Aww, you're all worried. That's so sweet."

Megan held the dress out persistently, and with a sigh, Anna got up and accepted it. "All right, since you care so much. But white is Jordan's favorite color."

Megan rubbed on peach lip gloss and ran a brush through her hair while Anna put on the black dress and finished her outfit with huge hoop earrings. Together, they walked down the steps of the cabin and headed toward the farmhouse. The sun was lower now, more golden than white.

The path widened to a piece of scratched-up ground with a low gray building in front. Through an open door came the sound of cooing birds. "Here're the chickens," Anna said. "We have to gather eggs twice a day, but watch out for the rooster. He'll attack your legs if he doesn't like your shoes."

Megan laughed. "No way."

"Seriously! You know my black wellies? He can't stand the sight of them. You have to make sure all the doors to the coop are shut and he's outside before you collect the eggs." They skirted the edge of the coop and neared the farmhouse. Megan could hear the babble of many voices as they approached. She swallowed. Anna must have noticed her sudden stiffness, because she took Megan's hand.

"Don't be nervous." Her voice was like a cool tonic on Megan's nerves. "Everyone will love you. And you know what? I'm going to pick out a guy for you tonight."

Megan stopped in dismay. "Anna, no, seriously! *Please* don't. I don't want a guy."

Anna waved her hand in dismissal. "Of course you do. That

way we can both have someone this summer." She squeezed Megan's hand. "You look gorgeous. Your hair is perfect like that. I mean it."

Megan smiled reluctantly. "Stop." But her voice lacked conviction, and Anna laughed as if she knew she'd won. She wrapped her arm around Megan's waist, and matching their footsteps, they went down the path together.

CHAPTER 3

In the side yard, the long picnic table was spread with a blue-striped tablecloth, which was anchored at each end with a large stone. Plates and yellow cloth napkins were stacked at one end, silverware in mason jars at the other. In the middle was a giant pitcher of iced tea, sweating moisture, and a cluster of tall glasses. The leaves on the big oaks rustled coolly, throwing their flickering green light over everything. The scene looked like some illustration of Classic American Farm Life, Megan thought. Subdivisions, four-lane highways, SuperTarget, and Starbucks felt very far away. It was nice. She was ready to be out of her old life for a while. It wasn't like there was anything particularly great back in suburban Cleveland.

As they walked up, Sarah came out of the kitchen with a big wooden bowl of salad. She had uncombed her braids, and her long, wavy hair hung down her back. Megan thought she looked beautiful. Sarah handed the salad to Linda, who was arranging items on the table. Dave, now clad in a shockingly bright red T-shirt, sat by himself on one of the benches, drinking a glass of tea and looking like he'd rather be back on his tractor. Thomas stood talking to two guys who were about Anna and Megan's age.

Megan stiffened at the sight of them and Anna nudged her in the ribs. "There! One of those is yours. Probably the bigger one."

"Nooo!" Megan hissed. The situation felt familiar. Anna was always picking out guys for Megan, but after a few minutes, it was usually clear that they preferred Anna instead. Anna would gracefully let it drop that she had a boyfriend, and then Megan would steel herself for the look of reluctance on the guys' faces as they turned to her, the second choice. Always the second choice.

"I don't see Jordan," Anna said anxiously just as Thomas waved them over.

"Girls!" he called. "Meet Robert and Isaac, the other summer hands. I'm sure you'll all enjoy working together."

"Hey." The guys nodded. Robert was hulking, with hands like softball mitts and a sheaf of blond hair falling over his forehead, while Isaac was thinner, with heavy dark eyebrows and a brooding expression.

"Thomas!" Linda called. "Can you light the bug candles?"

Thomas walked away and they all stood around in awkward silence for a minute. Megan crossed her arms in front of her chest, then uncrossed them, then clasped her hands behind her back. She wondered if her dress really did look like a granny dress. *Come on, Anna, say something.* It was like every party they'd ever been to. She was hiding behind Anna, as usual.

"So, have you guys ever worked on a farm before?" Anna asked, smiling easily.

"Hell, no," Robert answered. He had a big grin with lots of white teeth. "I never even had a pet. How about you? You ever worked on a farm?"

She rolled her eyes a little playfully. "Only, like, every summer since I was ten. This farm. But Megan's never been here before."

Megan jumped as Anna poked her in the side. "Um, yeah. I'm new too." *New too? How very Dr. Seuss of you, Megan.*

"Nice!" Robert's gaze fixed on Anna as if nailed there. "Isaac and me are freshmen at OSU. Our horticulture prof told us about this job. I worked construction last summer, so anything's better than that."

"Oh, Megan, you *love* horticulture, don't you?" Anna burbled.

Megan glared at her. Robert looked from one girl to the other as if trying to decode something.

"How about you?" Megan asked Isaac hurriedly. "Do you know anything about farms?"

He regarded her. "I've worked at the garden center some this year," he replied laconically. "So I know about plants. Not animals, though."

"We're almost ready to start, everyone," Sarah called across the lawn, wiping her hands on her jeans.

Megan headed toward the table with relief. It was obvious Robert could not be less interested in her, and she had no desire to prolong this torture. He wanted Anna, of course. Like always.

"Can you guys help move the table into the shade—*carefully*?" Sarah asked. The table was now loaded with platters of corn on the cob, carrots in some kind of cream sauce, green beans, a basket of rolls, cut-up watermelon, and bowls of vanilla and chocolate pudding. Megan's stomach gave a loud gurgle. She hadn't had anything to eat since her tuna sandwich on the bus.

"Megan?" Sarah went on. "Can you bring out the platter of chicken in the kitchen?"

"Sure." She nodded, glad for something to do.

The kitchen seemed dim after the outdoors, and Megan paused inside, letting her eyes adjust. It was a big, square room, with wooden cabinets lining every wall and old-fashioned wallpaper printed with butter churns and brooms. She glimpsed a living room through a doorway at the other end. The sink was filled with watermelon rinds and carrot peelings. In the center of the room, a long, dark wood table was wiped clean except for a dish heaped with fried chicken.

Megan leaned over and hefted the warm, heavy platter. The chicken was piled high, the top pieces balanced precariously. As she walked toward the door, her hip caught the high edge of the counter, rapping the bone sharply. She gasped, and the platter clattered to the floor. Chicken flew everywhere, skittering under the table and into the dusty corners of the room.

"Shit!" Megan whispered. Through the open window, she could hear laughter and conversation out on the lawn.

Megan dropped to her knees and picked up the platter just as she heard a toilet flush, then the sound of running water. A door opened at the other end of the room, and a tall guy with reddish blond hair and a two-day beard emerged. He stopped short in front of her, and Megan looked up from her kneeling position on the floor. For a moment, neither of them spoke. Then the guy said, "You know, I *like* my chicken with a little extra dust flavor." He bent down and picked up a drumstick.

Megan knew her face was scarlet. She scrabbled around, piling pieces of chicken onto the plate. "I wasn't watching where I was going," she mumbled. She could barely look the guy in the eye. She felt so stupid crouching there on the floor like a kid caught stealing cookies.

"Hey, don't worry about it," the guy said easily. He hunkered down on his heels and helped assemble the chicken. His hands were wide and bronzed from the sun. Little golden hairs sprinkled his forearms. Megan snuck a look at his face from under her eyelashes. He *had* to be Jordan. "I dropped an entire pitcher of sangria at my parents' twentieth anniversary party. I don't know why they were letting a ten-year-old serve the booze. There was red wine all over my mom's carpet." He held up the platter. "There. Not a dust bunny in sight."

Megan looked around. They'd gotten every piece. She sat back on her heels with relief. This guy was really nice. "Thanks so much." They both got to their feet. Megan paused, accepting the platter from Jordan. "Do you think it's . . . ethical to serve this?" She wanted to take the words back as soon as they were out of her mouth. *Ethical?* But Jordan didn't laugh, though the skin around his blue eyes crinkled at the edges as he looked down at her.

"Definitely not," he said seriously. "But I won't tell if you won't."

Megan laughed, and his face relaxed into a grin.

"Jordan, by the way."

"Megan, by the way." It was impossible not to smile back.

"Here, maybe you should let me take that out." He stepped forward to take the plate from her hands, and Megan caught a whiff of a cedary soap. For a moment, her breath caught. They were standing very close. He looked right into her eyes. The effect was piercing, intimate. Unbelievably, she wondered if he was going to kiss her. Then, in an instant, the moment was gone. Megan looked away as Jordan pushed open the door for her with one foot.

Megan hurried toward the picnic table where the others were assembled, fighting sudden guilt. *Stop, it was just one of those moments. He's not thinking about it anymore.* She gulped the glass of iced tea Anna placed in front of her, then held the cold glass to her forehead. Her friend touched her elbow.

"What's wrong?" Anna asked. "You're all pale and sweaty."

"I'm okay," Megan said as Jordan set the chicken on the table and slid onto the bench next to Anna.

"*Hi,*" Anna breathed, her face alight.

"Hi," Jordan said easily. He poured himself a glass of tea.

"Everyone, go ahead and start." Linda waved her arms over the spread. "Before the flies find it." There was a general clatter and shuffling as the serving dishes started going around.

"Pass the salad, will you, Dave?" Thomas asked.

Across the table, Robert was piling half the carrots onto his plate. "Oh, man, I love cream sauce," he announced to no one in particular.

Sarah passed Megan the corn. "So, Megan, where are you from?"

"Cleveland." Megan took an ear. It was bright yellow and firm, with big, juicy-looking kernels. She accepted the butter dish too and slathered on a big knifeful. "Actually, a western suburb." She paused. "This dinner is really different from the way we eat at home," she confided.

"Really? How so?" Sarah asked.

Megan thought of the usual Lean Cuisines, Kraft mac and cheese, tuna noodle casserole if her mother could find the energy. They had a table, but it was covered with homework papers and old mail. Dinner was eaten on the couch in front of the TV. "Dinner at home is, um . . . simpler."

Sarah nodded as if she understood what Megan was saying. "It's hard to cook a lot when you have another job. Taking care of the house and cooking is all I do." She gestured at the loaded table.

"Oh, no way!" Anna exclaimed on her other side. Megan glanced over. Anna had slid down several inches so that her shoulder was touching Jordan's as they ate. "You worked on a road crew last summer?"

"Yeah, we had to spread tar nine hours a day. It would get up to about one hundred and ten out there on the blacktop," Jordan was saying. "It had to be the worst summer job ever."

Anna squeezed his bicep. "That is amazing," she purred. "I think it sounds sexy." She tilted her head so her silky hair brushed his shoulder.

What? That doesn't even make sense. But Jordan didn't seem to care. Actually, he seemed pleased with Anna's obvious admiration.

"Can I have a bite?" Anna pointed at Jordan's bowl of watermelon with her fork and gave him a flirtatious glance. Megan saw Isaac raise one eyebrow.

"Sure." Jordan leaned back, and Anna stabbed a chunk of the pink fruit, raising it to her mouth and biting it seductively.

"—ever since college," Sarah was saying. Megan forced her attention back to the other conversation. "Dave loves it out here."

Dave nodded briefly from his spot at the end of the table and continued eating stolidly. Megan wondered if he ever talked.

"Where did you go to college?" Megan asked, trying to ignore Anna's buttery voice in her other ear. Now she was trying to feed Jordan a piece of watermelon with her fingers.

"Bryn Mawr . . ." Sarah trailed off, distracted by Anna. Isaac had actually stopped eating, and up at the head of the table, Linda pressed her lips together into a thin line.

Jordan ate the watermelon from Anna's fingers. She narrowed her eyes with satisfaction, letting her finger linger between his lips for a moment. Then Jordan noticed everyone was watching. A little flush rose in his cheeks.

Everyone resumed eating, and after the pudding had gone

around for the second time, Thomas stood up and cleared his throat above the busy hum of talk.

"I'd just like to officially welcome everyone," he said. "This summer will be busy, productive, and fun. And I hope you all are comfortable with manure."

The group laughed.

Thomas went on. "The daily work schedule will be given out each morning at breakfast and will consist of animal chores in the morning and evening, and garden work during the afternoons. There will be many other jobs in addition to the usual chores. My hope is that you each will choose an area of interest, such as the chickens, and focus on that for the summer."

Megan thought of Anna's tales about the rooster. She suspected that tending the chickens was not going to be her area of interest.

"Sarah is in charge of the kitchen, but the summer hands are expected to help out at meals. There is a schedule of kitchen duty on the fridge. Please check it so you know when you're assigned to cook and clean up. Robert, Isaac, and Jordan will have dish duty tonight, and Anna and Megan will do breakfast tomorrow." Thomas made to sit down, then stood again quickly as if he'd remembered something. "I know you all are aware of the abandoned section of the farm behind the sheep pasture. Let me reiterate that no one is to be back there at any time. The buildings are unsafe. Okay, that's it. Welcome to Given Farm, everyone!" He raised his iced tea glass in a toast.

There was a smattering of applause, then a general commotion as everyone stood up. Rosy sunset streaks painted the western sky, and twilight had already fallen in the shadows under the trees.

"Oh wait, everyone!" Thomas called out. He plucked an old-fashioned camera from the edge of the porch. "I like to get a picture of everyone on the first day—just a memento for you all. I'll have prints made for each of you."

"Aww, Uncle Thomas, you have a camera with *real film*?" Anna teased.

"I know, I'm such a throwback," he replied, herding everyone into position in front of the porch steps.

Megan found herself next to Jordan, with Anna on her other side. He winked at Megan as they all jostled closer together, then draped his arm casually over her shoulder. He smelled even better up close. On her other side, Anna was darting anxious glances at him.

"Smile!" Thomas clicked the shutter and the camera flashed.

The crowd broke up. Linda buzzed up the wooden ramp beside the steps and into the house, followed by Thomas, while Sarah and Dave headed to the pickup parked out front. A minute later, the roar of the engine retreated down the drive. Maybe they were going out to a bar or something. The boys began stacking the dishes and carrying them into the kitchen. Megan was warm and sleepy, full of dinner. She turned to the path that led back to the cabin, but Anna caught her by the arm.

"No, no!" Anna whispered. Her eyes gleamed in the semi-dark.

"What?" Megan asked irritably. "I'm tired. I want to go to bed."

"You can't. I have the best idea!" Anna pulled Megan behind a rhododendron as Isaac gathered up the last of the dishes and went into the kitchen, letting the screen door bang behind him. The lawn was deserted. Anna peered around the bush. "Okay. It's clear." She motioned for Megan to follow her.

Megan groaned as she trotted behind Anna across the grass. When they neared the house, Anna suddenly dropped to her knees and crawled toward the open kitchen window, which was a bright yellow rectangle of light glowing in the dark.

"Anna, this is stupid!" Megan hissed. "We shouldn't spy on them."

"Don't be such a mommy! I just want to hear if Jordan says anything about me."

They crouched below the window, their feet sunk in the soft soil of a flowerbed, and peered over the sill into the bright kitchen.

Isaac was standing at the sink, the water going full blast, washing a giant pile of silverware. The counter beside him was stacked with dirty dishes and serving platters. Robert was busy drying glasses with a flowered dishtowel. Another dishtowel was tucked into his belt like an apron, which Megan found oddly endearing. Anna's eyes locked on Jordan scraping chicken bones and other debris into the trash can. They had the radio on loud, but the windows were open and Megan could hear them easily over the music and the running water.

They were talking about Dave, Megan gathered after a moment. "—think he was working for Sarah's dad," Robert said. "Taking care of some thoroughbreds."

Megan felt Anna sag beside her in disappointment.

"Can we go now?" Megan whispered.

"In a minute." Anna held her arm. She moved closer to the wall and raised her head another inch to peer in. The deep blackness of the farm night pressed in, pinning them against the side of the house.

"Sarah's family has racehorses?" Jordan was asking. He carried another stack of plates over the trash can and kept scraping. "Are they really rich or something?"

Robert was opening random cupboard doors, looking for a place for the wooden salad bowl. "Sounds like it, right?"

There was a pause, then Isaac said, "Sarah's not bad." The silverware clanked against the side of the sink.

"Yeah," Robert agreed.

Outside, Megan stifled a yawn, her jaws aching, and let herself slide down the outside of the house, bracing her back against the siding. Her feet felt chilled and dirty. She thought longingly of the metal cot back in the cabin and wondered faintly when she was supposed to take a shower.

"Anna's hot for you, Jordan," someone said. It sounded like Isaac. Anna gasped and nudged Megan so hard she almost fell over. Megan eased her head up to the window again.

Jordan sat on the kitchen table now, elbows leaning on his knees. He laughed. "Yeah, can you tell?"

Robert giggled, a surprisingly high, girlish sound. "I thought she was going to jump you right there at the table." He snapped a dish towel in Jordan's direction. "You liked it, come on."

"Ehhh." Jordan shrugged.

Megan looked at Anna's face in the half light. Anna's lip trembled, as if she might cry.

It's okay, Megan mouthed to her friend, but Anna didn't seem to notice. She was focused on the scene within the kitchen.

Jordan continued. "Whatever, she's nice. Cute."

Anna drew in her breath sharply and her face lit up. She grabbed Megan's hand, digging her nails into the palm. "He does like me!" she whispered.

"Hey, you think we get to drive the tractor?" Isaac shut off the water.

"Yeah, that would be awesome," Robert agreed. Their voices faded as Anna pulled Megan around the house to the footpath. Megan could just make out the sides of the trail in the darkness. After a minute, her eyes adjusted and she could see ahead enough not to walk into a tree.

"Oh my God!" Anna squealed again as soon as they were away from the house. She clasped her hands in the middle of her chest. "Did you hear him?"

"Yeah, he said you were cute—that's great," Megan said encouragingly. "See? He does like you." A huge yawn almost split her head in two.

"But did you hear the *way* he said it?"

"What way? Hey, where do we take showers?"

"In the farmhouse in the mornings," Anna replied, then immediately returned to her favorite subject. "His voice was, like, so intense. He was feeling all these things he wasn't saying, you could just tell."

Despite her sleepiness, a little warning bell tinged some-where inside Megan's head. She slid a glance over to her friend as they walked. They were almost to the cabin. She could see its darker shadow against the trees. "Um . . . well, are you sure?" She kept her voice mild. "I wasn't really getting that."

"Yeah!" Anna said it as if talking to someone of limited intel-ligence. "Meg, you just don't know anything about guys, that's all. They never say how they *really* feel. You have to watch their body language."

Inside the cabin, Anna switched on the battery-powered lamp while Megan pulled her towel out of the trunk, draping it over her shoulder and grabbing her toiletry bag. "Will you come with me to wash up? I don't want to go out there alone."

With the light from the cabin window overhead, the night seemed darker than before. The air smelled of damp grass and, as they stood over the outdoor sink, the moldery odor of wet wood.

"So, what do you think of Robert?" Anna asked. She turned on the water, which spurted and ran reddish for a second before going clear.

"He could not have been less interested in me or more inter-ested in you. And he's totally not my type." Megan eyed the gray-ish soap on the end of the string and dug her soap case out of her bag. She gingerly splashed some water on her face. "This reminds me of camping."

Anna ran her toothbrush under the faucet. "Remember when my dad took us up to Raven's Gorge?"

Megan rubbed her fingers through the soap lather on her

face. "Yeah. What were we, like, eight? Remember we saw that skunk outside the bathroom?" She rinsed her face, then slurped a mouthful of water from her hands. She spit it out instantly. "It tastes like blood!"

"Iron and sulphur." Anna wiped her mouth on her towel. "It's springwater. You'll get used to the taste." She turned around and leaned back on the sink, crossing her arms while Megan brushed her teeth. "All those memories from when we were little—it seems like they happened to another person. Then Dad left and it was like I could really see the world for what it was. A place where you're all alone."

"But you still had me," Megan reminded her around her toothbrush.

Anna's mouth turned down, but she nodded.

"Yeah. I felt like you were the only person I could trust after that."

Megan tried to read a hidden meaning in Anna's words, but Anna just raised a finger to her mouth and chewed her nail absently. Megan gathered up her soap and bag, and the two went back inside the cabin. Megan's body was aching for bed. Dumping her toiletries back in her trunk, Megan padded over to her cot and climbed in between the sheets. She'd pulled the covers up to her shoulders and turned on her side before she realized that Anna was still standing in the middle of the floor. The weak yellow light of the lamp threw her face into deep relief—her eye sockets like pits, her cheekbones like hills, shadows at the corners of her mouth.

"I saw the way you looked at Jordan tonight, Megan."

Megan drew her breath in.

"You might as well face it, Megan," Anna said quietly. "He's in love with me. It's obvious."

Megan swallowed, which was audible in the utter quiet of the cabin. "That's so awesome. I'm really happy for you." If only she could believe it was true.

"You should be. You of all people should be."

CHAPTER 4

Megan twisted the stiff shower knob and stuck her hand under the spray. Cold. She waited a minute. Still cold. Groaning silently, she put her towel down on the sink and turned the knob again, this time with both hands. She was rewarded with spluttering and then, gradually, warmer water.

Pulling back the crinkly shower curtain, Megan carefully stepped into the deep tub. It was one of those old-fashioned ones with feet, the kind you could practically swim in.

Megan tilted her face to the spray, letting the water wash off several layers of sweat and grit. She could hardly believe she'd woken up yesterday morning in her own bed. So many things had happened since then.

Last night had been particularly long—the wool blanket felt scratchy, and she'd kept swiping her feet against each other under the covers just to make sure there weren't any little animals hanging around under there. The racket of frogs and insects outside was deafening, and it went on *all night*. Whoever said country living was quiet had obviously never actually been out *in* the country.

Megan had slipped out of bed, head pounding, dying to rinse off her sticky skin, as soon as the sky began to lighten. On the other side of the room, Anna had slept with annoying soundness, lying on her back with her mouth open, hand relaxed on her chest. Megan had located her towel, which she'd left outside on the sink last night, so it was damp, and had picked her way down the muddy path to the house.

Now she shut off the water, toweled off, and pulled on clean jeans and a T-shirt. She wrapped her hair into a knot and stuck a long bobby pin in it before opening the bathroom door.

Dave and Sarah leaned on the counter, wearing faded flannel bathrobes and watching the coffeemaker as it burbled, filling the room with its nutty fragrance. Two blue mugs sat waiting. Their hands were touching in what felt like a private moment. Megan wondered if she should slip back into the bathroom.

But before she could, Sarah turned around. "Oh, hi! Morning. You sleep okay?" She smiled and Megan relaxed. Sarah didn't look annoyed at the interruption.

Dave nodded hello and Sarah went on. "You're on breakfast duty, right? Today, it's eggs and toast and fruit. Everything's in the fridge or on the counter. Just figure two to three eggs per person."

She poured coffee for herself and Dave, and the two of them

wandered over to the table. Megan stood uncertainly in the doorway for another minute before she realized those were all the instructions she was going to get. This was going to be interesting. She was more of a cold cereal girl at home.

After some fumbling in various cupboards, Megan found a huge black frying pan and started cracking eggs into a blue bowl. She'd just reached twelve when the screen door opened and Anna came in, wearing yesterday's cutoffs and one of Megan's T-shirts, her face still puffy from sleep. She was followed closely by Robert and Isaac, both with hair that looked like it had been whisked. The boys collapsed at the table, immediately burying their heads in their arms, while Anna started sticking slices of bread in the toaster.

"I borrowed your toothbrush this morning, okay?" Anna said in between yawns.

"Where's yours?" Megan scraped at the pan. The eggs were starting to stick. She glanced over at Sarah, hoping for some help, but Sarah was talking to Isaac.

"Don't know. Maybe I dropped it last night. I had the craziest dream. We were all at this party in some basement and—" She stopped as Jordan entered the kitchen, looking only marginally more awake than the others. He was wearing a faded gray T-shirt and a pair of jeans with dirt embedded in the knees. The red-gold stubble on his chin and cheeks glinted in the sun streaming in through the windows.

Megan's heart rate immediately increased. She was blushing for no reason and forced herself to look at the frying pan, hating herself for reacting like this when all he'd done was walk into the room.

She scraped fiercely at the pan with the spatula. This batch was done. She dumped the eggs onto a plate and started a second batch. *Just ignore Jordan. Pay no attention. He's just a guy, like the rest of them.* Except somewhere deep in her mind she knew he wasn't. He was different.

Anna slid a plate in front of Jordan with two slices of hot buttered toast slathered with jam. Jordan looked down at the plate, then looked up and down the bare table. There was a little pause as everyone watched. No one else had any food.

"Um, thanks," Jordan said. "Toast, anyone?" Then he turned to Robert. "You were snoring all night, bro. Isaac and I took turns poking you—do you remember that?"

Robert guffawed. "No, I always sleep like a horse. Nothing bothers me."

Eat like a horse, Robert. The expression is "eat like a horse," not sleep like one. Megan suspected Robert might not be the sharpest knife in the drawer, as her grandmother used to put it.

Megan stirred the eggs with the spatula, and a half-cooked chunk slopped out of the pan. She winced and grabbed a sponge from the sink.

Anna noticed, of course. "Eww, Megan," she said. "Those can be yours." Megan flushed at Anna's loud tone and shot a glance toward Jordan, who wasn't paying any attention. She focused on stirring as the familiar anger at Anna welled up, then subsided. Really, it wasn't any different from how Anna always treated her.

Except that it seemed worse with everyone—okay, with Jordan—sitting right there.

Thomas tramped in near the end of the meal, carrying the scent of the outdoors with him. His sleeves were rolled to the elbow, and his hands were stained with grease. A large monkey wrench stuck out of his back pocket. "Hello, all," he said in a cheery voice. He was obviously one of those people who loved mornings. But that was probably a requirement for all farmers.

Thomas bustled around the kitchen busily, fixing himself a cup of coffee. Then he pulled a list out of his pocket. Megan pushed her eyelids open wider. Farm work was great in theory, but the big breakfast had made her sleepy, and what she really wanted was to wander back to the cabin and take a postbreakfast nap.

Thomas leaned back against the counter and perused his list with relish. "So, this morning, we're going to have Robert and Isaac feeding and watering Samson, throwing hay to the sheep, feeding the pigs and mucking the pigsty, and collecting eggs." He looked at the boys. "You boys will have to take the hay to the sheep in the truck. You know how to drive a stick?"

Robert nodded.

"Megan, Anna, and Jordan will do the horse barn."

"Okay," Megan said. She glanced at Anna, who preened as if she herself had made the assignment.

"Feed, dump and scrub water buckets, strip the stalls, scrub, and put down fresh shavings," Thomas told them. "Also, please groom both horses and the donkey. Check their feet, turn them out, and sweep the barn aisle and the feed room. Throw down two flakes of hay to each horse, one for the donkey. This will take you up to lunchtime, if you're doing it thoroughly." He looked at his niece. "Anna will show you where everything is. She's done the job a few times."

"A few!" Anna rolled her eyes in mock exasperation. "Try a hundred. You're such a slave driver, Uncle Thomas."

He laughed. "Dave and I will be out harrowing the oats most of the morning. I'll come by to check on you all, see if you have any questions." He waved at them as he headed back outside.

There was a general scraping and chattering as everyone pushed back their chairs and carried their dishes to the sink. "I've got dishes," Sarah said.

"You guys want to walk over together?" Jordan asked.

Megan felt almost blinded by his gaze as he smiled at them. She tried to reply, but her throat was suddenly dry. She coughed. "Sure," she managed.

"Great." Once again, he met her eyes square on. Heat zinged through Megan's belly. She cut her eyes away fast and turned to the table, stacking up random silverware, just to give her hands something to do. She prayed Anna hadn't noticed the moment.

But her friend was beaming up at Jordan. "Of course we can walk together," she simpered. She didn't take his arm as they all clattered down the porch steps, but she might as well have.

The air outside smelled freshly scrubbed. As they passed the garden, the pumpkin vines and tomato stakes were silvered with moisture. A gentle mist lingered near the ground, hiding in the low places as if it were reluctant to leave, despite the steadily brightening sun. Megan felt like she'd never really *seen* any of these things before, like she had super-vision now that she was on the farm and could notice things like the tiny balls of dew on the grass. She watched a finch hop up to a puddle and hesitate at the edge, like a tiny diver, before jumping in.

"Look!" Megan said before realizing that she was alone. The others had gone ahead—Robert and Isaac were just disappearing into the shed where the pickup was kept, and farther down the path, she could see Anna holding Jordan's arm and chattering to him as they walked. Jordan's shoulders were straight and broad, his back narrowing to his waist in a V. Megan forced her eyes away. *Anna's boy. Anna's boy. Anna's boy.* What was *wrong* with her?

Megan caught up with them at the barn. Jordan rolled back the big double doors, and the fragrance of sawdust and horses wafted out. Minuscule bits of hay floated everywhere, and overhead, swallows swooped in and out of the hayloft. One of the horses—Darryl, Megan thought—whinnied at them as they came in, and the donkey did a couple of excited little turns in his stall.

"Why is he dancing around like that?" Megan asked Anna.

Anna opened a door near the front of the barn. Inside was a tiny room lined with metal trash cans, each clearly labeled. She cast Megan an impatient look. "He wants his breakfast." She didn't say "idiot," but she might as well have.

Megan flushed and glanced at Jordan, but he was studying the hose in the corner and then starting to unravel the green loops.

"Hey, you girls want to start feeding and I'll do the buckets?"

Anna smiled at him. "Great idea."

Megan peered into the garbage cans. Each held a different kind of grain.

"Okay, show me what these guys get for breakfast," she said. "Anna? Anna!" Her friend was still watching Jordan uncoil the hose.

"It's really sexy watching guys work, don't you think, Megan?" she said loud enough for Jordan to hear.

Megan grabbed a big steel scoop from the wall. "Focus, Anna. Here, do we use this to measure it out?"

Anna dragged her attention away from Jordan. "Hmm? Uh, yeah. It's this feed here, the sticky stuff. Half scoop for each horse. Cisco just gets a handful."

"Okay." Megan dumped the grain into a smaller bucket nearby and carried it out to the stalls. Both horses pricked their ears eagerly at the sight of the bucket.

"Hi," Megan said softly as she approached. Rosie bobbed her head up and down as if responding. Her belly looked even bigger this morning than it had yesterday. Megan carefully reached over each horse's half door and emptied their grain into their feed bins.

"Here, Meg," she heard Anna call. She turned, and her friend pitched her a currycomb. "Brush Rosie while she's eating. I'll do Darryl. Then we can turn them out and do their stalls. You just rub in circles from neck to tail."

Megan slid back the bolt and slipped into the dimness of Rosie's stall. The mare seemed huge up close, but Rosie ignored

Megan, keeping her head sunken in her feed bin as she eagerly snuffled up her grain.

Jordan appeared at the door to unclip the heavy water bucket, then moved on to Darryl's stall. Gently, Megan started currying the mare's neck, moving the currycomb against the short chestnut fur. The skin was warmer under the horse's heavy blond mane. Rosie continued eating, and Megan rubbed in steady circles, feeling the firm muscles under the horse's skin and watching the dust puff under her comb as she worked. She felt like she was cleaning her mind as well. Rubbing out all Anna's little jabs from yesterday and today. Rubbing out the sight of Anna's face in the dark cabin last night. A memory floated up of a time a few summers ago when Anna had been in one of her moods. She'd come over to Megan's house to tell Megan exactly why she found her so annoying. She'd sat in Megan's room, calm, complacent, spelling out the reasons while Megan cried tears of impotent rage.

Finally, Megan had screamed, picked up a wooden-soled clog from the floor, and thrown it at Anna's head as hard as she could. It had missed and broken the window instead. Megan licked her lips. She hadn't thought of that for some time.

"Are you excited for your baby?" she murmured to Rosie to distract herself. "You're going to be a mama."

The horse flicked an ear at the sound of her voice. Megan worked her way along the horse's back, and Rosie leaned against her hand as if appreciating the massage. Megan scratched her around the base of the tail, which her dog always used to like, and then started brushing her flanks.

Her reverie was broken by a splash and Anna's squeal from the next stall.

"Jesus, I'm sorry," Jordan said.

Megan stuck her head over the half door. Anna and Jordan stood just outside Darryl's stall. Anna was holding the water bucket, and the front of her T-shirt was soaked with water.

"I'm so sorry," Jordan repeated. "I didn't realize you were trying to take it from me and—"

"No, it's my fault," Anna interrupted. "It doesn't matter anyway. I have another shirt on underneath."

She set down the water bucket and slowly, as if she were in a movie, peeled off her T-shirt, revealing a strappy pink camisole that barely concealed her lacy cream bra. Jordan watched, mesmerized, his mouth open a little, while Anna shook out her hair.

From Anna's triumphant look, Megan knew that the water spill had been no accident. She felt a surge of jealousy, knowing that she herself would never have the nerve to try a move like that, but she quickly squashed the feeling. It didn't matter what Anna did around Jordan, Megan told herself fiercely. She was *Anna's friend* and that was all. She *owed* it to Anna to help her get Jordan.

Jordan swallowed hard then and glanced at Megan as if suddenly aware of her presence. "Um, hey, should we clean the stalls now?" He addressed the wall between the two of them.

"Sure," Anna replied, still smiling. "I'll just take these guys out to the pasture."

Megan and Jordan watched in silence as Anna walked the

horses down the wide barn aisle, one lead rope in each hand. The donkey trotted closely behind.

Megan looked at Jordan, wondering if he liked watching Anna walk away in her damp camisole. She caught him glancing at her at the same moment. He rolled his eyes a little as if to say, *What was that?*

Megan smiled. Jordan grabbed a pitchfork leaning against the wall and handed it to her, then took one for himself. Together, they started lifting out piles of manure and wet bedding from Darryl's stall. It was weird, Megan thought, how she'd barely talked to Jordan since meeting him yesterday, but she felt like she'd known him for years. Like he was an old friend, someone you knew so well, you didn't have to talk all the time when you were together. She watched him work quickly, efficiently, hurling forkfuls of dirty bedding into the wheelbarrow with a quick flick of his wrist. Suddenly, she laughed in spite of herself. He looked up.

"What?"

"It's just that you look like you've done that before. Did you grow up on a farm or what?"

Jordan laughed a little. "Sort of. My parents have some land near a little town by the Michigan border."

"Which one?" Megan worked her fork under a particularly intimidating pile of manure.

"Lodi? It's this little place—"

Megan straightened up. "I totally know Lodi! My mom used to go up to the outlet malls there all the time on our way to Detroit."

"Oh, yeah, I forgot about those." Jordan scraped at some wet bedding stuck to the stall floor. "We're even farther off the highway. Most people who go up to the outlets don't make it into Lodi itself. I mean, I don't know why you would if you didn't live there." He sent her a sideways look. "How about you? You're from Cleveland, right?"

"Yeah, unfortunately." Megan tried to keep the loaded fork steady.

"Why unfortunately?"

"Oh . . ." Megan laughed a little. "My area is all ugly subdivisions, very suburban, very plastic. You know the kind of place. The Lakes of Crystal Pointe, that sort of thing."

"Cool." He sounded like he was thinking about something else. He cleared his throat. "Do—um, so did you leave your boyfriend behind back there?" The words got a little strangled in his throat.

Megan shot him a startled look. He was spreading the manure in the barrow with great concentration.

"Um, no," she said slowly. "I don't have a boyfriend right now." *Or ever.* "How about you?" She felt like she was taking a step toward some unknown precipice. Trespassing on dangerous ground.

"No." He looked at her, his face open and his eyes clear. "With any luck, I thought I might meet someone this summer." The words fell between them, like pebbles scattered from a bucket.

"With any luck . . . ," Megan repeated. Unconsciously, she moved toward him an inch.

Then she jerked herself back. *Stop. Stop. Stop.* She grabbed the shovel and started scraping Rosie's stall with unnecessary vigor. "So how come you're not working on your family's farm this summer?" Her voice came out louder than she intended.

"Aww, that's so cute, your parents are farmers?" Anna came up beside Jordan. She was pushing another wheelbarrow, this one filled with fresh pine shavings.

Jordan closed his eyes briefly, as if gathering himself, then opened them. "No, they're not. Not really. I'll tell you guys about it some other time. It's kind of a long story." He concentrated on scraping out the corner of Darryl's stall. "So, how long have you guys been friends?" he asked, changing topics.

The moment is gone, Megan thought, *as if it never existed.*

"Too many years to count," Anna said, going into Rosie's stall. "Since we were in first grade."

"Yeah, Blair Haymont wouldn't let me jump rope with her, and Anna came to my rescue. I was sitting out with the recess monitor, and Anna came up and hugged me." It was the first of many, many times that Anna had saved her from social ruin. Megan brushed at some shavings that clung to her sweaty cheek. It was getting hot in the barn. "Did Thomas say we had to hose the stalls?"

"Yeah, he told me earlier." Jordan lifted a rubber mat at the bottom of Darryl's stall and shook it out in the barn aisle.

"I'm always rescuing her!" Anna called from behind the partition. A second later, she appeared, dragging Rosie's rubber mat, which she flopped next to Darryl's. "Just yesterday, I had to save her from getting trampled by Samson." She grinned at Megan.

"That might be a *slight* exaggeration." Megan kept her voice light. It was true that Anna was always rescuing her, but she didn't have to make her look stupid in front of Jordan.

"But, Jordan, the worst, the absolute worst, was when I *tried* to stop her from going to the winter formal last year with this complete nerd. She wouldn't listen to me." Anna giggled, looking from Megan to Jordan and back again.

Megan stopped shoveling. She stared at Anna standing there in her skimpy shirt with her silly expression. *How dare she bring up that fight and those memories like it's just another funny anecdote.*

"Oh, yeah?" Jordan's back was turned as he screwed a nozzle onto the green hose. "What happened?"

"Well, it was around last Christmas," Anna began. Her voice was bubbly and intimate, full of the promise of a good story. "And Megan had been going out with this guy, Laurence, who was just so icky. I *told* her he was icky. He had pimples all over the back of his neck, and his face was always red and scraped up with razor burn." Anna gave a pretend shudder.

Anger rose up strong and thick in Megan's throat. How dare Anna pick at old scabs like this? Laurence had always been a sensitive topic and Anna knew it. She'd been really good about not bringing it up before, as if she sensed Megan didn't want to be reminded of it. *She* would never do this to Anna, Megan thought furiously as she grabbed the handles of the full wheelbarrow. Well . . . except for Mike. But that was a mistake, and she'd apologized a thousand times already.

"This really needs to be dumped," Megan said, and pushed the wheelbarrow off without looking at either of them. If Anna was really going to dredge up that story, Megan would rather not be around to hear it. She remembered it perfectly well on her own.

Megan had gone out with this guy Laurence for just a few weeks, and he *was* a giant nerd. He had a long neck and a little head kind of like a dinosaur, and wore T-shirts with BAMA on them all the time, which he never failed to inform people was for the University of Alabama, where he was from. Megan had kind of liked him and was kind of ashamed of him too, which she knew was wrong, but she couldn't help it.

Anna, on the other hand, had had no such conflict. She thought Laurence was a complete dork and would not let up about him. The remarks had been nonstop, especially after Megan had told her that Laurence had asked her to the winter formal and she was thinking of saying yes.

Anna had made some comment about his lips, which *were* kind of thick, like a girl's, and Megan had finally snapped, telling Anna to shut up—shouted at her, actually—which she'd never, ever done before.

Megan would never forget the look on Anna's face. Anna had gone utterly blank, then started sobbing. Her hair had been hanging in her eyes, snot running down her face, saying she thought Megan was the only person who loved her, but she must have been wrong, and now she had no one. Then she'd yanked at her own hair so hard that Megan thought she was going to rip fistfuls right out of her scalp.

Megan had apologized immediately, hugging Anna and reassuring her that she was there for her, always. Laurence had sprained his knee a week before the dance, and after that, he hadn't really seemed worth all the fuss.

Megan gritted her teeth at the memory. The sun was high in the sky now, and its glare beat down on her head as she struggled to tip the last of the manure from the wheelbarrow. The horses had wandered to the far side of the pasture and stood together, heads to the ground, tails switching. Megan wished she had a tail. There were flies buzzing everywhere. She was sweaty, her hair was falling out of its ponytail, and she really wanted a Diet Coke. With a grunt, she flipped the wheelbarrow upright and wiped her forehead with her arm.

Anna's voice greeted Megan as soon as she reentered the barn. Anna was leaning over the half door of Cisco's stall, resting her arms on the edge while Jordan scrubbed the floor with a huge brush.

"—and my dad left when I was ten," Anna was saying.

She must have finished the Laurence story. Megan wondered if Jordan thought she was as big of an idiot as Anna was making her out to be.

Jordan got to his feet as soon as Megan set down the empty wheelbarrow. He took a clean, folded bandanna out of his pocket and wet it with some water from the hose, offering it over the stall door to Megan.

"Here. You look hot." He shook his head, flustered. "I mean warm. You know what I mean, right?"

Megan took the bandanna, placing it on the nape of her neck and letting trickles of icy water run down her back. "Thanks."

"No problem." He held her gaze for a second longer until she dropped her eyes, confused. Damn it, there it was again. And in front of Anna, too. Was he flirting? Or just being nice? Did Anna see it?

But behind them, Anna fiddled with Cisco's feed bucket, trying to detach it from its clip on the wall. She finally yanked it free and, emerging from the stall, handed the bucket to Jordan. "Can you come get sweet feed with me?" She deliberately let her fingers caress his as he took the bucket. "I want to leave Cisco a little treat, but there was a mouse in there before."

Megan turned away and forked some clean shavings into Rosie's stall. There was no mouse, of course. The door to the feed room closed with a thump. Megan shoveled shavings faster, trying not to mind that Anna was surely making out with Jordan right now. *Why should I mind? Okay, so the guy had amazing eyes and an unnervingly direct gaze. Whatever. He's not yours! What the hell is wrong with you? You almost lost her once, Megan. Don't let it happen again. What kind of nasty bitch crushes on her best friend's boy one day after meeting him? This. Will. Not. Be. Another. Mike.*

At the same time, Megan knew Anna was acting out of control. Seriously, there was no need to make out with Jordan right here, right now. Couldn't they at least sneak around after dark like normal people?

Still, she has a right to do what she wants, she reminded herself. *He does too.* It was none of her business anyway. Maybe if she told herself that enough times, she'd actually start believing it. The shavings barrow was almost empty now. She'd need some more for Darryl's stall.

Back out to the big open shed on the outer wall of the barn. Shovel the clean white shavings. Back inside. Don't look at the feed room door. Don't listen. Listen to what? Maybe they really were filling feed buckets. Megan fought a mental picture of Anna and Jordan, half-undressed, entwined on a pile of feed sacks. She shoveled the rest of the shavings with furious speed, gripping the handle of the fork so hard her knuckles were white. *In addition, I'm doing all the freaking work here, on the first day*, she thought bitterly. *Thanks, Anna. Thanks.* Maybe this was her penance. Maybe Anna thought she hadn't been punished enough over the last year. Maybe Anna was right.

Megan heard a door open and fixed her eyes on her pitchfork, which moved steadily between wheelbarrow and stall, leaving a little white trail of shavings with each scoop.

Footsteps. She turned around. Her stomach plunged when she saw they were holding hands—no, Anna was holding *his* hand—and Jordan's ears were pink. Well, that was that. He was into her. *As he should be. Anna deserves this, and you know it.* Anna looked flushed and satisfied. It was the way she used to look when she'd gotten into shoplifting their freshman year. Her lips were red at the edges.

Jordan didn't look at Megan. Instead, he grabbed the manure wheelbarrow and pushed it away, mumbling something about dumping it, even though it was empty.

"Thanks for sticking me with the work," Megan said to Anna

when Jordan was out of earshot. "Have fun making out in the feed room?" She kept her voice casual.

"I wasn't the only one having fun." Anna raised her eyebrows significantly. "I'd say he was having a pretty good time too."

Megan felt a little twist of pain in her gut. She tried to keep her face neutral as she grabbed a broom leaning nearby and began sweeping the barn floor. "So, things are working out?" *Maybe she would say no. . . .*

"You could say that." Anna's voice was soft, and Megan glanced over at her friend, who was sitting on an overturned mud bucket with a dreamy expression on her face. All of a sudden, Anna looked just the way she used to when they were younger, when they would search for four-leaf clovers or make fairy meals on plates of leaves. Megan's turbulent feelings about the Jordan situation, the hurt at Anna's verbal jabs, all of that evaporated, leaving Megan only with the fresh realization that this was her oldest and dearest friend—and she was in love, or something pretty close to it. Megan knelt down beside Anna.

Anna looked at Megan full in the face. "I really like him," she said simply.

Megan nodded. "He's nice. More than nice—"

"Sitting down on the job, girls?" a voice interrupted.

Thomas stood in the far doorway of the barn with Rosie on a lead rope and Jordan beside him.

Megan jumped to her feet as they approached, but Anna remained sitting.

"I've been sitting here all morning, Uncle Thomas, while

these two did the work," she declared, mischievously.

Thomas didn't even blink. "If that was the case, you'd be on the first bus home, dear. But I know you better than that. Is Rosie's stall ready?"

"We just finished," Megan said. "Is she . . . feeling okay?"

Thomas led her into the fresh, sweet-smelling stall and took off her halter. "Well, she's not sick, if that's what you're asking. But she is in early labor."

The girls gasped and clutched each other in excitement. "How do you know?" Megan asked. She looked at Rosie, half expecting her to drop to the floor and produce a foal that instant.

Thomas ran his hands lightly over the horse's bulging sides. "I stopped to check on her while she was in the pasture. She's showing the usual signs, but it could be awhile yet. You know what that means. . . ." He looked at Anna.

"Foal watch!"

"What's foal watch?" Jordan asked.

"Oh, it's so much fun! You stay up all night and watch the mare and just hang out, eat snacks, and talk, and then, if the foal starts coming—"

"Come and wake me up," Thomas said. "I don't think she'll do it before morning, but we'd better play it safe." He ran his fingers over his short white beard. "Let's see. Dave has to go over to Tractor Supply real early tomorrow, and Sarah's on breakfast duty. They need some sleep tonight, so we'll leave this to you summer hands. Let's have Megan and Jordan do the first shift, then Anna and Robert after that. Isaac can take the prebreakfast watch if there's no foal by then."

They all nodded. Megan actually clapped her hands. An actual foal, born right here in this barn! This was probably the most exciting thing to ever happen to her. She pushed aside the equally thrilling thought that she'd be alone with Jordan for her shift.

When the others had gone ahead to lunch, Megan lingered behind to pat Rosie's nose once more.

"Are you scared, girl?" she asked the mare. Rosie chewed a mouthful of hay. Her big dark eyes looked calm. She was probably used to this. Megan tried to remember if Thomas had said she'd had babies before, or if this was her first. She scratched behind Rosie's ears.

"Well, if you're worrying, don't," she told her. "Someone will be with you the whole time. You won't be alone."

Anna stuck her head back through the barn doors. "Megan. Come on, dweeb! Everyone's already eating."

Megan gave Rosie's nose a last pat and hurried to the door. She felt all quivery with anticipation, thinking of the upcoming night. "I'm starving," she told Anna outside. "What's for lunch, do you know?" She started down the path, her stomach rumbling, but Anna grabbed her hand.

"Wait, I have to ask you something," she said.

Ahead on the farmhouse lawn, Megan could see everyone seated around the long picnic table. Sarah was standing at the head, talking, holding a platter aloft in one hand, gesturing with the other. Megan thought she could smell meat. "What?" She made as if to keep walking. "I think they grilled burgers."

"No, listen. Wait just a second." Anna spoke in a hushed tone, even though no one else was around. "Switch shifts with me tonight. You can hang out with Robert and I'll be with Jordan."

Megan stopped and groaned. "I thought we were done with the whole Robert plan. Seriously, I am so not into him, and the feeling is definitely mutual." Secretly, she knew her protests weren't all about Robert.

"No, come on, you have to!" Anna pleaded. "I'll think up some excuse for Uncle Thomas—I'll tell him I can't stay up that late. He won't care." She clasped her hands like a little girl. "Please, please? Oh, come on, Meg, this is my chance with Jordan! You know, to show him how I really feel."

"Your *chance?*" Megan couldn't resist snorting. "Didn't you have your chance in the feed room just now?" She started walking again.

"Come on, Meg, *please?* I really need your help." Anna's eyes were huge.

Megan sighed. "Fine."

"Thank you!" Anna squealed and kissed Megan on the cheek. "I love you."

Megan grimaced. "You should."

They were almost to the lawn now. The pleasant hum of voices and the clink of silverware on plates floated toward them on the breeze. Everyone was squeezed together around the long table, spooning out potato salad and green beans. Sarah spotted them and called out, "Come on, girls, I saved some burgers for you."

"Coming!" Megan called, just as Anna's hand grasped hers and pulled her back.

"Just look at him," Anna whispered, her breath blowing hot against Megan's ear.

Megan watched Jordan lean over to refill Linda's water glass. His hair shone in the sun like spun gold. *He is beautiful*, she thought. She wanted him so badly, she felt like screaming. But she didn't, of course. She just remained silent.

Anna moved forward as if drawn by an invisible thread. "It's going to be a great night," she murmured.

CHAPTER 5

"Oh my God, I am so red," Megan moaned later that evening as she stared into the tiny, smeary mirror that hung on the cabin wall. The little room was hot and stuffy after being shut up all day, but they'd propped the door open, and a cool breeze was finally beginning to blow through.

"Didn't you put on sunscreen?" Anna asked, sitting cross-legged on the bed and pulling a brush through her heavy black hair.

"I sort of forgot." Megan switched on the lamp and dug a jar of aloe out of her toiletry bag. "Good thing Mom stuffed this in my bag at the last minute." She unscrewed it and gazed at the green goo inside. "It looks toxic."

Anna started to plait her hair into a long braid. "How was weeding? Hey, do you want me to braid your hair? It looks so pretty like that."

Megan smiled. "Yeah, that'd be nice. Thanks." She sat on the floor between Anna's knees and let her friend pull a comb through her tangled hair. It felt very peaceful, very familiar. Megan thought back to all the times she and Anna had sat like this, with a comb and a mirror, over the years. Too many to count.

"Anyway, weeding was fun. I mean, hot, but it was nice," Megan resumed. "Isaac and I did most of it, but Sarah came out and helped some, and Linda sat and talked to us. She made me put her hat on when she saw how red I was getting." Megan peered at her reflection and started smearing aloe on her burnt nose.

Anna sniffed, dividing Megan's hair into three sections. "She's always in other people's business like that."

It took Megan a moment to realize that she was talking about Linda. "It wasn't like that. She was just trying to be nice. She told us a bunch of stuff about the farm too. Hey, did you know she and Thomas were one of the first farms in the *state* to go organic? Everyone told them they'd never make it, and they did."

"Yeah, I think I knew that." Anna skillfully wrapped a hairband around the end of the braid and smoothed a few stray pieces. "Okay, done."

Megan got up and stared at herself dolefully in the mirror. Her hair looked nice, and her skin was no longer green from the salve, but it was shiny. Shiny, wet, and red. She put the aloe away and lay down on her bed, adjusting the pillow behind her neck, and watched Anna rummage in her trunk, holding up various tank tops, then discarding them. "Seriously, why don't you like Linda? She seems really nice to me."

Anna shook her head vigorously. "*Seriously*, she's a bitch, okay? Trust me. I've known her a lot longer than you." She pulled an emerald green tank over her head, mussing her long braid, which somehow made it look even better. Anna seemed to be considering something. Then she sighed.

"Okay, fine. Listen, when I was eleven, I spent the summer up here. It was right after Dad left, and I was really pissed off all the time. That summer, they had this big old dog, Nigel. I think he'd come with some sheep they'd gotten. He was kind of cranky and smelly, but Linda just loved him. I loved him too. I used to talk with him like he was the only one who could understand me." Anna paused, sitting down on the bed, her hands dangling limply between her knees.

Megan pushed herself up on her elbow. "And?" she prompted.

Anna sighed. "And one day, Aunt Linda went off on me because I said I'd fed the pigs and I hadn't. We had this big fight. Uncle Thomas told her to go easy, that my dad had just left us, and she said that didn't matter, work was work, blah, blah, blah.

"I just lost it, listening to all the yelling, so I found this rope and put it on Nigel and ran down the road with him." She laughed a little ruefully, as if watching her teary eleven-year-old self. "But he pulled away and a car came by and hit him."

"Ohh," Megan breathed. "That's awful."

Anna wiped under her eyes. "I know, right?"

Anna shrugged. "Aunt Linda's had it in for me ever since." She got up from the bed abruptly and put on her sandals. "But it doesn't matter. She was a bitch before, too." Her mouth was hard, and she stared at the wall for a long moment. Then she blinked, and her whole face changed, as if someone had pulled up a window shade. Anna's eyes sparkled and she smiled radiantly at Megan. "Hey, do you think Jordan will tell me he loves me tonight?"

"Um . . ." Megan struggled to shift gears. "I don't know. Does it seem like he . . . does?"

Anna looked at her like she had three heads. "*Yeah.* Anyway, I want to be the first to say it."

Megan watched her friend pick up a bottle of perfume from the bedside table and squirt her neck. Megan cleared her throat. "Maybe you should wait a little. That's a big step. I don't know if he's totally ready." *Please, Anna, don't get hurt. Please be careful.* No matter who it was, she couldn't stand watching Anna make herself so vulnerable, like she always did with guys, and then have her heart broken. Just like Mike, Jordan *didn't* love Anna. Megan knew that. She could just sense it, and she had to protect Anna—*from* Anna, really, not from Jordan. *And if it doesn't work out, Megan, are you saying you'll just forget Jordan ever existed? You won't try to grab him for yourself? Why, that's very selfless of you.* No. No. That wasn't even an option. Not after last summer.

Anna scowled. "I don't even know why I asked you. You don't know anything about guys." She patted her hair, eyeing Megan in the mirror.

Megan said nothing.

"Okay, wish me luck." Anna swept out the door, leaving the scent of lemon in her wake.

"Luck," Megan whispered to the empty room.

The cabin was quiet after Anna left, despite the chorus of cicadas and peepers that started up outside. Moths hurled themselves frantically against the screen door like kamikaze pilots. Megan stripped down to her sports bra and tried to read a book her mother had given her before she left, *The Moon and Sixpence* by W. Somerset Maugham. The story was pretty good, but her wool blanket seemed to be made of a thousand prickles. She squirmed and scratched until she could tell she was getting all splotchy.

Finally, Megan heaved herself upright and grabbed her watch. It was only eleven. Another hour to go until she was due for her shift. She wondered what Anna and Jordan were doing. *No, don't think about that. It doesn't matter, it doesn't matter! Remember your resolution. Stay out of Anna's business. Rosie. Think about Rosie.* She wondered how the mare was feeling. Maybe the foal would be born before her shift. No, Thomas had said she probably wouldn't go before morning, Megan comforted herself. He would know, after all.

Soothed by this thought, she dug a long-sleeved T-shirt from her trunk and pulled it on, then lay back on the bed again and tried to concentrate on Maugham. The words were blurring in front of her eyes, though, and massive yawns kept splitting her jaws.

Megan didn't realize that she'd fallen asleep until she felt a hand on her shoulder and opened her eyes to see a large, bristly face bending over her. "Oh!" she shrieked, and tried to push herself upright before she realized it was Robert.

"Hey, sorry! You were sleeping." He grinned.

Megan ran her tongue around her cottony mouth, trying to wake up. "Yeah, I know." She swiped at some dried drool at the corner of her mouth. "I'll meet you on the porch in a few minutes, okay?" she said deliberately.

Robert looked confused for a second, then his face cleared. "Oh, yeah. Okay." He lumbered outside, and Megan heard the creak of the steps as he sat down.

Retreating into a corner away from the door, she took off her T-shirt and pulled a gray hooded sweatshirt over her head. She stuffed her flashlight into her back pocket and, after a moment's hesitation, swiped on a little rosy lip gloss. Who it was for, she wasn't sure. Rosie, maybe?

Robert stood up as she came out onto the porch. "Ready?"

She nodded, and they started down the path toward the chicken coop. There was no moon, so the only light came from a mess of stars flung across the sky. The horizon held none of the orangey glow Megan remembered from the city. Here, the blackness was total.

Robert insisted on walking right beside her, forcing Megan partially into the weeds at the side of the path. At the farmhouse, the porch light burned brightly, but the upstairs rooms were dark. They skirted the house, and as they came out onto the drive Robert cleared his throat. It sounded like gravel rattling in a metal trash can. "Um, you know Anna?"

Megan smothered a giggle. "Yeah, I think I know her." She sensed what was coming next.

"So . . . is she *officially* with Jordan?" He was concentrating on the path.

Megan tried to speak gently. "Well, not officially . . ."

They were passing the fence line of the pasture. "Do you think she'd, you know, go for me?" Robert's voice was hopeful.

"Well . . . I think she's pretty into Jordan right now."

"Listen," Robert said with a touch of urgency, "you're her best friend. Will you put in a good word for me?"

"Sure," Megan said, giving up.

"Thanks."

The two approached the barn doors, and Megan was about to slide one open when Robert slapped his hand to his forehead.

"I forgot my water bottle. Hey, do you care if I run back real fast?"

Megan shrugged. "Fine with me."

Robert pulled his flashlight from his pocket and disappeared around the side of the barn toward the guys' bunk. Megan rolled the heavy door open just enough to slip through.

Most of the barn was in shadow, but a few of the lights were switched on down by the horse stalls. "Hey," Megan called softly. "How's Rosie?"

No one was visible, though she could hear Rosie shifting in her stall. Thomas had told them that Darryl and the donkey would stay outside for the night, so that they wouldn't disturb Rosie by banging around or whinnying.

Megan looked around. There were a couple of chairs pulled up by the stalls, with a paperback book lying facedown on one.

Megan walked over and looked at it. *Pilgrim at Tinker Creek*. An open can of root beer sat beside it.

Rosie stood calmly in her stall, her head drooping. Megan didn't think she looked any different from the way she had that morning.

"How do you feel, girl?" she asked the mare, who half closed her eyes. *Pretty good*, Megan guessed, since she was basically falling asleep.

There was a rustle behind her, followed by a giggle. Megan turned. The door to one of the empty stalls was ajar. *Damn it. Damn it!* She paused uncertainly in the middle of the floor until another giggle floated out. Okay, she wasn't going to stand here and *listen* to them make out. She had a shred more self-respect than that. Steeling herself, she walked over to the stall.

Jordan and Anna lay sprawled on a pile of straw, Anna half-draped on top of Jordan, her shirt on the ground beside her. She was giggling, trying to pin Jordan as he held her shoulders away from him. "I'm too strong for you, Jordan," Anna said, laughing. "I've got you. . . ."

"Hey, whoa there, Anna—" he said, but she wasn't listening. Instead, she reached down, trying to kiss him. Megan could see Anna's hands go to his belt buckle before Jordan finally managed to lift her off of him.

Anna sat back on her heels, blowing her hair out of her face, still laughing. Just then, she caught sight of Megan standing by the door.

"Oops!" She grabbed her shirt and held it up to her chest in a gesture of modesty that Megan could see she didn't mean one bit. Jordan's face flushed scarlet, and he got hastily to his feet, brushing off his clothes. He looked horribly embarrassed.

"Hi," he mumbled, and strode past Megan without looking at her.

Anna couldn't seem to stop giggling as she fumbled for her sandals, which she'd apparently kicked off, and her sweatshirt.

"I am so crazy about him!" she whispered as Megan went over to help her up. Anna's voice held a tinge of mania. "He's so, so sweet. Listen, listen to my plan—"

"Come on, Anna, shhh. He'll hear you. Just put your clothes back on. Robert's going to be here any second." She picked some straw out of Anna's hair. "Don't you think you're moving a little fast?"

Anna sighed through her nose and pulled her shirt over her head. "No, silly! Everything is perfect, okay? Don't worry about me." She swept from the stall and Megan followed her, wishing she didn't have to see Jordan. She wanted to erase the whole stall scene from her mind, but she kept seeing their bodies together on the floor.

But wait a minute, Megan, a little voice asked in the back of her head, *wasn't he trying to push her away?* But he was in the stall with her! *Still,* the little voice argued, *you don't know what she told him to get him in there.* Either way, did it matter? No. All that mattered was keeping Anna from making a fool out of herself.

More lights turned on down by Rosie's stall. Robert and Jordan peered over the door, excited.

"Hey, something's happening!" Jordan pointed.

Rosie had moved to the middle of the stall, and the hair on her neck and shoulders was now dark with sweat. She was champing her jaws and occasionally stomping her feet. Her eyes were wide and her nostrils dilated. Every muscle in her body was tense.

"Oh, wow!" Megan grabbed Anna's hand and felt her friend squeeze back. All the weirdness from before evaporated. It was like they were nine years old again, about to go on the biggest roller coaster at the amusement park.

"Someone'd better go get Thomas," Jordan said.

"I will." Megan grabbed her flashlight and ran from the barn, her feet pounding on the path's hard-packed dirt. She prayed Rosie wouldn't have the baby before she got back. How fast were baby horses born?

She banged open the door to the farmhouse harder than she meant to, wincing at the noise, and ran up the stairs, trying not to thump too loudly.

At the top of the stairs, Megan was confronted with three closed doors—and realized she didn't know which one was Thomas and Linda's room. She knocked softly on the nearest one, then opened it and saw a sink and a tub. Not that one. She cracked the door of the next room and made out Linda's wheelchair on one side of the bed. She could see the outline of Thomas's beard on one of the pillows. The sound of deep breathing filled the room.

Megan crept over to the bedside. Thomas made a little whistling noise every time he breathed, like a teakettle about to boil. Gently, Megan shook his shoulder.

"Thomas," she whispered.

Nothing. She shook a little harder.

"Thomas."

"Hmm-what?" He stared at her a moment, then swung his legs over the bed. Linda mumbled something and rolled over. Thomas quickly pulled a pair of overalls over his red and blue striped pajamas. "How far along is she?" he muttered as they crept from the room.

"I don't know," Megan said. "She's breathing hard and really sweaty."

"Standing up or lying down?"

"Standing—or at least, she was standing when I left."

Thomas opened the front door. "Okay. Good thing you got me so quickly."

They hurried down the path and back into the barn. Someone had switched on all the lights, and the brightness was dazzling after the darkness of the night sky. Robert and Jordan were pacing up and down like expectant fathers, while Anna stood at the stall door.

"Uncle Thomas, she just lay down," she called. "Hurry!"

Thomas opened Rosie's door. The mare was stretched flat on her side on the clean shavings. The skin on her belly had taken on a strange wrinkled appearance.

Thomas knelt by the mare's side, and she let out a deep, long groan. Megan sucked in her breath and groped for Anna's hand again.

"Is she dying?" she whispered. "She sounds so awful."

"I don't think so." Anna's eyes were reassuringly steady. "Look—Uncle Thomas isn't worried."

Thomas calmly stroked the horse's neck and murmured to her. Rosie went into a prolonged strain, her mouth wide open.

Megan's heart hammered and she squeezed Anna's hand as hard as she could. It was so intense, she wanted to look away, but she couldn't. The barn was silent except for Rosie's panting. The mare groaned, louder this time, and strained again.

"Look!" Jordan pointed. A tiny pair of hooves were visible under the horse's tail.

"Oh my God!" Megan squeaked, excited and grossed out at the same time. She and Anna grabbed each other, hiding their faces on each other's shoulders. Megan peeked out of one eye and through her lashes as a glistening dark head and shoulders emerged, draped in a whitish membrane. The rest of the foal followed in a rush of fluid.

And then, just like that, Rosie raised her head and heaved herself over onto her chest. The foal was already snorting and struggling, trying to figure out his legs.

Thomas pulled the foal up to Rosie's head. She immediately began nuzzling and licking it from head to tail.

The five of them watched, riveted, until Thomas rose stiffly and brushed the shavings from his knees.

"A little colt," he said with a huge grin. They were all grinning actually, standing there in a line in front of the stall as if they'd just watched the Kentucky Derby. The foal was drying off, his thick newborn fur fluffing out. He was chestnut colored, like Rosie, with a wide white stripe down his nose.

As they watched, Rosie stood up, then reached down and nudged the foal with her nose. He staggered to his knees and then, with a visible effort, climbed to his feet.

"All right!" Jordan said. Megan felt like there should be a blast of trumpets. Her throat swelled and she felt tears prickle her eyes. She did her best to blink them away. No one else was crying, but she did see Jordan give her a quick sideways glance. She smiled at him briefly, hoping he wouldn't notice her shiny eyes.

Thomas led Rosie to a neighboring stall with fresh bedding and a full bucket of water. The foal followed, testing out his wobbly, knock-kneed legs.

"Let's give Rosie some privacy." Thomas ushered the group toward the door. "We'll scrub the birthing stall in the morning."

Outside, they paused near the barn doors. They weren't high-fiving each other, but Megan felt like they should be. There was a general sense of "good work, team."

"Get some sleep," Thomas instructed. "Isaac and I will do the morning chores." He patted Anna and Megan on the shoulders. "I'm glad you two could be there. I know how much you were looking forward to it."

The guys went around to their bunkhouse, and Anna and Megan walked slowly back toward the farmhouse with Thomas. Now that the excitement was over, Megan's feet were heavy. But the fatigue felt good. Thomas waved good night on the porch.

Megan and Anna trudged up the path to their cabin in silence for a while. "Are you thinking about the foal?" Megan asked.

Anna paused. "Of course," she said, and linked her arm with Megan's for the rest of the walk.

It was only later, when she was cocooned in the rough comfort of her bed, that Megan realized Anna had been lying.

CHAPTER 6

"Well, I thought it was icky." Anna sat on her bed, her back against the wall. Funyun crumbs covered the black tank top she had slept in. She stuffed another handful into her mouth, then folded over the top of the bag and attempted to pitch it across the room to Megan, who lunged over the edge of her mattress to catch it. She missed, though, and Funyuns sprayed over the cabin floor.

"Damn it." Megan climbed out of bed and started picking up the greasy onion rings.

It was eleven and they still hadn't left the cabin. The day outside was gray and cloudy. There was no breeze. They probably would have emerged sooner if Anna hadn't had a snack stash in her trunk. Still, Megan was starting to feel like she needed to brush her teeth. "How can you say it was icky? It was, like"—she searched for the proper words—"the miracle of life!"

Anna slurped from the can of warm Diet Coke beside her. "A

nasty miracle. All that blood and whatever else was coming out of her—I don't even want to know."

Megan located the last renegade Funyun under the bed and tossed it out the open door. She went over to her trunk and dug out some clean underwear and her second-to-last pair of jeans.

"Well, I thought it was amazing." Megan almost choked up all over again, just thinking of Rosie nuzzling her new baby. "What was really incredible was how fast the baby got up. When you think about human babies and how helpless they are . . ." She threw her clothes on the bed and pulled off her pajama top.

Anna grinned. "Hey, how'd you like hanging out with Robert last night? He's not too bad, right? I told you you'd like him." She waggled her eyebrows suggestively.

Megan tried not to let her annoyance show on her face. "Hah-hah. He's into *you*, for your information. He told me so last night." She yanked her Cleveland Indians T-shirt over her head.

"I've already got my boy." A secretive look crossed Anna's face. She beckoned Megan closer, then stuck her hand under her pillow. She pulled out a square of gray cloth and dangled it before her.

"What's that?" Megan took the cloth in her hand. It was a piece of jersey material, about the size of her palm. The edges were jagged and uneven.

"Promise not to tell?" Anna leaned over, even though they were alone. "It's a piece of Jordan's shirt."

"*What?* What did you do?"

"Nothing." Anna snatched the swatch and held it against her

chest. "I was just playing around. I snuck up behind him yesterday while he was trying to fix the hose and cut it off the bottom of his shirt."

"You *cut* it off his shirt?" Megan stared at her. "Did he notice?"

Anna shook her head. "He had no idea. That razor is really sharp."

"Jesus, Anna. I can't believe you're carrying that razor around with you." Megan knew her voice was rising, but she couldn't help it. "Are you crazy?"

Her friend's brow darkened. "I should've known you wouldn't understand. You're always such a priss." She paused. "Except that one time, of course."

Megan swallowed as silence filled the cabin. She looked out onto the porch, where a squirrel was busy shucking a walnut on the steps, then back at her friend. "I'm sorry. I shouldn't have called you crazy."

"I just want to keep a piece of him near me," Anna said. "That's all." She kissed the cloth and slid it inside her shirt. "I'm going to wear it here, always. Right next to my heart." She pressed her hand over the place where the cloth was.

The air in the cabin suddenly felt unbearably close.

"Okay, yeah." Megan stuffed her feet into her sneakers. "Hey, um, I'm going over to the barn. See how the foal's doing . . ."

As her sneakers padded along the muddy path, Megan pictured Anna creeping up behind Jordan and silently, delicately, slicing a piece off of his shirt. Then she thought of Anna's face in the cabin just before. Flushed. Intense. Mr. O'Gorman's handsome, swarthy face swam up in front of Megan's eyes as if conjured there. It was four years ago now, but the memory gave her the same crawling feeling she'd had at the time.

Mr. O'Gorman was nice, and cute—the cutest teacher in the school, in fact. Lots of girls had had crushes on him. During American history, half the girls passed notes back and forth, talking about his shaggy hair, his green eyes, the way he'd sit on his desk when reading aloud to them. But Anna took it to a different level.

First, there had been the whole T-shirt thing. After all the fallout from that, Megan had been ready to back off from the Mr. O'Gorman Fan Club, but Anna wasn't. She'd talked about him all the time. It had been hard to get her to focus on anything else. Anna had stolen her mom's credit card and paid for some online site, just so she could get his unlisted phone number. After that, she'd called his house every night to hear his voice and hung up when he'd answered.

And she'd written him these long letters, which she'd kept in a special velvet bag she'd sewn. Anna had stolen his red coffee mug after class one afternoon when he was in the faculty lounge. Megan knew because Anna had shown it to her. She'd held it against her cheek and then stood on her tiptoes and pushed it onto a high shelf in her closet where her mother wouldn't find it.

And Megan was the only one who knew that Anna had ridden her bike over to Mr. O'Gorman's house every weekend after her mother had fallen asleep. She sat outside, watching his bedroom window.

She couldn't see much, Anna had told Megan later, because he always had his shades down, but just watching his shadow walk back and forth was enough.

It had all blown up when Mr. O'Gorman had finally had the phone calls traced. Anna had to have a big meeting with her mother and Mr. O'Gorman and the principal and Ms. Seaver, the guidance counselor. The upshot of the whole thing was that Anna was transferred out of Mr. O'Gorman's class and put on probation for the rest of the year.

Megan stopped abruptly in front of the barn. The memories were boiling up inside her, threatening to drown out any excitement at visiting the new foal. She shook her head, trying to clear her mind. This wasn't middle school, she told herself. Jordan wasn't Mr. O'Gorman. And it wasn't any of her business what Anna did. She could take care of herself. She'd told Megan that plenty of times.

The barn doors were open, but no one was inside. The doors to the horse stalls stood ajar, and shavings and hay were strewn in front of Rosie's stall. Megan went through to the open doors at the other end and found Thomas, Dave, and Isaac leaning on the fence, watching Rosie cropping grass in the pasture while the foal lay by her side. He wasn't moving, and Megan's heart skipped an instant before she realized he was just sleeping. Darryl and the donkey grazed nearby.

"Hi," she said, coming up to stand beside Isaac. "How's the baby doing?"

"Beautifully," Thomas told her. He was wearing fresh overalls and a blue denim shirt. "Rosie's a natural mom." He dug in his pocket and handed her a white envelope. "Here's the photo from yesterday. There's one in there for Anna too."

"Hey, I hear you got to see the whole thing," Isaac said, smiling his little sideways smile. "Congrats. Not sure I would've wanted to see it myself."

"Actually, it was incredible," Megan told him. "A little . . . messy, but incredible."

Dave snorted and Megan blinked in surprise. She never thought she'd be the one to make Dave laugh.

"Megan, I have a job for you, if you'd like," Thomas said. "You remember I had mentioned that I hoped you would each find a project to work on this summer, apart from the usual chores."

Megan nodded.

"How would you like to start training the new foal?"

Megan tried not to shriek in excitement. "Seriously? Wow. That would be so, so amazing. I mean, I feel like I know him already." She squeezed the top rail of the fence to keep from throwing her arms around Thomas.

"Isaac and I are going to go muck out the pigs," Dave interrupted. Megan guessed he wasn't too interested in her raptures over the foal. Isaac gave her a little wave, and the two strolled off. As Megan watched them go, her stomach suddenly sank.

"Um, Thomas?" she asked hesitantly. "I don't really know anything about horse training."

He didn't look concerned. "That's okay. This part, the early stage, is more about getting the foal used to people." He put his fingers in his mouth and whistled across the pasture, two sharp blasts. Rosie looked up from her grazing and trotted over, her tail held high. The foal climbed to his feet and ran beside her like a shadow. Darryl and the donkey followed behind.

When the mare and foal came up to the fence, Thomas rewarded her with a piece of carrot he had pulled out of his pocket. Darryl and Cisco tried to push in, but Rosie flattened her ears and warned them off.

"She's feeling a little protective," Thomas explained. He patted the foal firmly on his fuzzy head. "Basically, I want you to get the baby used to being handled. Every day, you'll brush him, pick up each of his feet, get him used to wearing a halter. Once he's comfortable with all of that, you'll want to teach him how to walk on a lead rope. That'll be about it until he's a year old or so."

"Okay," Megan said slowly. The foal's brown eyes were startlingly human. "That doesn't sound too hard." She reached out and patted the baby's head too.

Thomas gave her an encouraging smile. "It's not. It just takes patience and kindness. I see that in you, Megan. You've got a quiet way about you that the horses like." He plucked a tiny red halter off the fence post beside him and handed it to her. "You might as well get started."

Megan took the halter. The sun was peeking out from the clouds, and it shone bright on Thomas's white hair. Several yards away, he stopped and turned around. "By the way," he called, "think of a name, will you?"

A *name*! Megan turned back to the mare and foal, who were

both still standing expectantly at the fence, probably waiting for another carrot—or the mare was, at least.

The pasture felt empty without Thomas's confident presence. Even the scrape of the gate latch seemed loud as Megan drew it back. It felt funny being in the pasture with the horses, instead of in the stall. Too open, somehow. She walked over to Rosie and patted her neck. The mare sniffed her hands, and finding no carrots, dropped her head to the grass.

Megan looked at the foal, who gazed back at her curiously. She cleared her throat.

"Hi," she said. She reached out and touched the little horse's mane, which stood straight up. The hair was soft, not coarse like Rosie's. Megan half expected the foal to shy away from her, but instead, he reached out with his delicate upper lip and snuffled her shirt.

"Hey, now," Megan gently pushed the little nose away. At least he wasn't afraid. *Okay. Thomas said to get him used to being handled.* Megan fetched a currycomb and brush from the barn and returned to find the horses standing under the shade of a big tree in the corner of the pasture. She slipped under the fence and, talking softly to the foal, started rubbing him with the currycomb, taking off the last bits of muck from the birth. The little body felt unbelievably delicate in comparison with when she'd groomed Rosie. Instead, the foal seemed to be strung together entirely out of tendons, fur, and long bones.

The baby liked the brushing, Megan figured, since he was leaning on Megan's hand, but he was curious about the black rubber comb and kept reaching around and trying to bite it.

"No, no," she told him quietly, and gently pushed the foal's head so that he faced the front. Meanwhile, the foal kept stepping this way and that, as if he were ticklish. The squirming reminded Megan of trying to get her two-year-old cousin dressed when she babysat him.

The clouds overhead were breaking up in earnest now, scuttling away in big gray clumps. A haze hung over the grass, and the air was humid and mellow. The donkey was asleep standing up in a shady corner, but the horses switched their tails constantly and stamped their feet as they grazed.

Megan switched to the soft brush. The baby liked that even better than the currycomb. Megan managed to brush his whole body, even down his long, slender legs, talking to him the whole time. He seemed to like that—his ears flicked back and forth.

As she worked, Megan realized she hadn't thought of Anna once since she stepped into the pasture. Her mind had been entirely occupied with the little horse, but in a calming way, like meditating. It was a relief—she didn't realize how tense she'd been, watching Anna's movements, analyzing her moods, trying to figure out the Jordan situation.

"There you go, sweetie," Megan cooed. She tried to keep her voice low and steady. She set the brush down on the fence rail and ran her hands along the baby's spine. "Does that feel nice, sweetie?"

The foal turned his head and looked right at Megan. He had beautiful long eyelashes. "Maybe that should be your name," Megan told him. "Sweetie. Do you like that?"

She half waited for the foal to reply, but instead, Megan heard a horn beep behind her. Anna and Jordan bounced up the road in the old truck, with Jordan at the wheel. Anna hung half out the window, waving her arms at Megan.

"We're going to feed the sheep. Come throw hay with us!" Anna's cheeks were bright red, and she was wearing a loose linen shirt with half the buttons undone.

"Hang on," Megan called back. She gathered the brush and the comb and gave the foal one last scratch before slipping under the fence. She trotted over to the truck, which was chugging noisily and belching out smoke from its tailpipe. Several bales of hay were piled in the back, along with a sack of grain.

Jordan greeted her with a friendly smile. "We could use the extra hands." His teeth looked very white in his tanned face, and he was wearing a much-washed blue shirt with the sleeves rolled to the elbows, showing off his corded brown forearms. Megan caught a whiff of the same cedary soap he was wearing Monday night.

Anna leaned over, almost lying across his lap. "Come on, Meg! Jump in the back." She pushed herself upright, putting her hands on Jordan's thighs and letting her hair graze his face. He swallowed.

Megan looked from one to the other. "Are you sure you guys want company?"

"Definitely!" Jordan said, his voice a little overenthusiastic.

"Okay."

Megan hoisted herself into the bed of the truck and perched on a prickly hay bale as Jordan threw the truck into gear and bounced them down the rutted road. The pigs were rooting around in their feed trough, grunting low in their chests and half climbing on each other to reach the choicest bits as they drove past. Megan pulled the collar of her shirt up over her nose. None of the other smells on the farm bothered her so far, not even the donkey, but the pig manure was in its own special category. She was happy to have avoided feeding them so far.

The truck bumped off the gravel and onto the grassy track that circled the sheep pasture. Jordan followed the fence around to the back, passing the abandoned part of the farm, before stopping at the sheep gate.

The pastures unrolled before them, steep and hilly. The sheep grazed together at the far end of the field, but the air smelled strongly of sheep dung. It wasn't as bad as the pig manure, though.

As she and Anna wrestled the bag of grain out of the truck and staggered with it toward the feed trough, Megan felt strong and tough in an earthy-girl kind of way. Back in Cleveland, she never had the chance to throw around fifty-pound sacks of grain. It felt awesome, actually. She'd always thought of herself as a physically wimpy kind of person, someone who needed two hands to pour a gallon of milk. Now she relished the strain in her shoulders and hands as she and Anna let the big bag thump to the ground.

Anna ripped open the top of the grain bag, and together she and Megan hoisted it, pouring the little round pellets into the trough. The sheep began trotting over, drawn by the smell of the food. They bleated and jostled each other to get to a place. Megan had to push her way through the flock, their pillowy wool pressing up against her calves.

Jordan pulled a hay bale from the back of the truck. He looped his hands under the orange twine that bound it, and with a heave, flung it over the top of the fence. For a moment, Megan stood still, transfixed by the play of his shoulders under the thin shirt. Then she shook her head and glanced at Anna, who was also watching him.

"You guys want to relax there a little longer, or are you going to help spread this around?" Jordan called.

"We're helping," Megan replied. Meanwhile, Jordan flung another bale, then climbed over the fence and took what looked like a blunt metal hook from his back pocket.

"What's that?" Megan asked.

He stuck it on top of one of the twine loops and held it vertically, then began twirling it like he was twirling spaghetti. "Hay hook. Dave showed me how to use it. You just keep twisting and—" The orange twine broke under the pressure and sprang off, releasing the bale.

Megan laughed. "Why not just cut it?"

Jordan shrugged and stuck the tool in his back pocket. "I don't know. Maybe they don't want us summer hands wandering around with knives."

Megan flashed on Anna's pearl-handled razor. That would have cut the orange strings all right. She wondered if Jordan had noticed his torn shirt. Megan started separating the flakes of rough hay and spreading it over the grass. Anna carried an arm-ful over to the sheep at the trough. The hay smelled dusty and green, like her gerbils' cage used to smell. Suddenly, there was a scuffle behind her and a burst of laughter.

"Hey!" Jordan exclaimed.

"Got you!" Anna shrieked.

Megan turned around. Anna had crept up behind Jordan and stuffed a huge armful of hay down the back of his shirt. Now she was grabbing at him with new fistfuls and giggling.

"It's going down my pants! Damn, that's prickly." Jordan pulled his shirt up, dumping most of the hay out, and scooped up an armful of his own, eyeing Anna and stalking toward her like someone hunting prey. "Oh, you're going to get it now. Just wait."

Anna hopped away, holding her arms out. "Oh, no. No way," she stammered between laughs.

Jordan lunged for her, but Anna feinted left, then right, evad-ing him. Megan snickered as she watched. Jordan turned sud-denly, catching her standing close by. "Hah! Got you!" He snared the hem of her shirt and stuffed the hay down her collar.

Megan shrieked theatrically and tried to grab him to retali-ate, but he darted away and she tumbled to the ground. Then Anna ran up and dumped another armload onto Jordan's head.

"Hey!" He flung some at Anna. Then she tried to run away but tripped on Megan's still-prone body. They lay there, sprawled on the bed of hay, laughing too hard to talk, while Jordan flung himself down nearby.

Their laughter turned to gasps, broken only by the occasional giggle as Jordan propped himself on one elbow, grinning at them and chewing on a hay strand.

"Oooh." Megan sighed. "My stomach hurts." She combed a handful of hay from her hair with her fingers.

"Me too," Anna said. She sat up and then pointed. "Look!"

All twenty-five sheep were standing in a ring around the three of them, their eyes bright and interested, as if they were watching a tennis match. Megan dissolved into giggles again. The sheep scattered as the three got to their feet and headed back to the truck in companionable silence, picking hay from their clothes.

Megan sat on the remaining hay bale in the back, while Anna and Jordan climbed into the cab. Anna drove away from the pasture. Megan leaned back, letting the warm metal of the truck bed soak into her back. She wondered if they were going to get any lunch today, since it was already past two. Maybe Sarah wouldn't care if they made sandwiches to take with them to afternoon chores. She was on the verge of knocking on the back windshield to ask Anna to stop at the farmhouse, when the truck stopped with a jerk. Megan had to grab the edge of the bed to keep from being flung forward.

She looked around. They were by the old barn. Overgrown pastures sloped down and away from the abandoned buildings. At the bottom of the pastures, woods began, a thick, dark mass of trees and honeysuckle bushes.

Anna hopped out, followed by Jordan.

"What's up?" he asked. "We're not supposed to be back here."

Anna's eyes were alert. "Pretty please? I just wanted to look around a little. I've never really been back here." She started off toward the barn. Jordan glanced at Megan and she shrugged.

"We can't let her go by herself," Megan said. "It could be dangerous back there." They hurried after her.

The knee-high grass caught at Megan's legs as if trying to hold her back. She tripped on something at her feet and gasped, looking down. The rusted metal rods of some piece of farm equipment lay concealed in the long grass like a forgotten skeleton. Megan broke into a half run until she caught up with Jordan and Anna at the doorway of the big barn.

"Anna, wait." Megan tried to catch her breath. "Thomas said we weren't supposed to be back here."

"*Thomas said*," Anna mimicked without turning around. She peered into the darkness inside the barn. "Why don't you walk back if you're so worried about what 'Thomas said'?"

Jordan put his hand on Anna's arm. "Look, Anna, let's just go back and—"

But Anna shook off his hand and darted ahead. After a second, her voice came echoing out. "This place is incredible, you guys."

Megan and Jordan exchanged another look as they went inside.

Anna was standing in the center of the huge, soaring space, her neck craned up, her hands on her hips. "This place is huge," she said as they entered. "It's three times the size of the horse barn. Look how high that is." She pointed up, where the ceiling was lost in shadows. Sunlight filtered through holes punched in the roof.

The old barn was a monument to the ravages of wind, rain, and snow. One half of the roof sagged dangerously. Megan took a step, and the floorboard sank noticeably and groaned. She had the distinct sensation that if she took one more step, it would give way completely.

"Anna, come on," she pleaded. "This place isn't safe. Seriously, the floor's about to cave in." A rustle came from a nearby corner, and Megan whirled around. Something with wings flapped off through a hole in the wall.

A bird. A bird, Megan told herself. *Just a bird.* She stepped through the gloom and gently took Anna's arm.

"Come on, let's go." Megan gently tugged on Anna's arm. This situation felt very familiar. Anna about to do something seriously wrong. Herself talking Anna down. Megan flashed on the time in third grade Anna thought they should climb the school fence and go home for lunch. Anna had been straddling the top of the chain-link and Megan had been tugging on her leg, trying to get her back down, when the lunch monitor had caught them.

"Yeah, let's go get some food," Jordan chimed in. He sounded uneasy. The barn had a chilly, faraway feel, as if they'd stepped sideways into another world. Megan could tell Jordan was as anxious to leave as she was.

Anna freed herself and strolled over to the row of broken windows. They gaped, lined with jagged glass. The stall dividers had fallen over on one side of the barn, like a row of dominoes, and the air was sour with rot. Pieces of rusting machinery were strewn around, and the carcass of a discarded plow hulked near the opposite doors. Cobwebs hung like dirty lace on every surface.

Anna fished something from the floor at her feet. "Oh, look," she said. She held what looked like a claw up to the light. From where she stood, Megan could see that it was rusty and sharp.

"Anna, put that down," Jordan said. "It's a piece of an old tool."

But Anna didn't turn around, not even at Jordan's plea. She stood by the window, turning the claw this way and that. Then, abruptly, she flung it to the floor, spun on her heel, and started walking rapidly around the perimeter of the barn, her face alight. "Don't you guys just love this? Such a sense of the past in here. I don't know why Uncle Thomas is so uptight about it."

"Hey, don't you want to go make sandwiches?" Megan asked, hoping to distract her. "I'm craving tuna fish for some reason."

"Yeah, we'd better get the truck back," Jordan said at the same time.

Anna stopped walking. "What the hell? Are you two ganging up on me?" Her eyes darted from Megan to Jordan and back again.

"No, no," Megan soothed Anna. "I'm just starving. And this place is giving me the creeps."

Anna sighed and rolled her eyes, but she allowed herself to be led from the barn, casting a backward glance over her shoulder. Megan felt her own shoulders relax as they walked back to the truck.

Before getting in, the three of them paused, standing side by side, looking down the long slope at the abandoned pastures.

"This quiet *is* nice," Jordan said. "So much nicer than the road noise I had to listen to all last summer on the tarring crew." He grinned. "Plus, you girls are way nicer to look at than those ogres." He squeezed Megan's shoulder briefly and climbed into the truck.

Megan felt her shoulder tingling where he'd touched it. Then she realized Anna was watching her. Megan tried to smile, squashing down a little worm of guilt suddenly wiggling through her.

"Ready?" she asked Anna tentatively. Her friend turned her gaze down the hill toward the dense woods at the end of the abandoned pasture.

"Sure," she said after a long pause.

Megan turned for the truck when she felt something hit her solidly in the lower back, knocking her off balance and almost sending her tumbling down the slope. She rocked forward, pinwheeling her arms, and then caught herself, whirling around. "Did you push me?" she demanded of Anna.

Her friend knelt on the ground, holding her knee. Anna looked up, and Megan was surprised to see tears in her eyes.

"No, bitch," Anna said, gritting her teeth. "I just tripped on a stone and totally banged up my knee. Thanks for standing right in front of me like that."

"I'm sorry." Megan looked closely at the knee but couldn't see any visible scrapes or bruises. Anna winced with pain but shook off Megan's hand.

"Jordan will help me," she snapped. "Jordan!"

He stuck his head out through the truck window. "What? What happened?"

"My knee's hurt." She sounded like a sad little kitten.

Anna limped as Jordan helped her to the truck. But the injury must have been fleeting, because by the time they got back to the farmhouse, Anna leapt out of the truck as lightly as a deer.

CHAPTER 7

It was Dave and Sarah's morning to cook, and the kitchen was filled with the scent of frying bacon when Megan and Anna stumbled in the next morning. Megan spotted blueberry pancakes through her half-opened eyes. She collapsed at the table, and Anna sank down beside her. Aside from Linda sipping her coffee at the head, they were the first ones in. Megan tried to appear perky, resisting the urge to lay her head on the table.

"Good—" She yawned. "Good morning, everyone," she managed.

"Hi," Sarah replied, turning from the stove. Beside her, Dave lifted thick slices of bacon from the black skillet and lay them to drain on layers of paper towels.

Linda looked amused. "You'll get used to the six o'clock wake-ups before long," she said. She wheeled herself a little closer to the table and pushed the platter of pancakes down toward them. "A treat for you girls—you're going to have a busy morning."

Anna didn't respond. Instead, she gave Linda a cool stare, then stuck her fork through an entire stack of pancakes and dumped them onto her plate. She drowned them in half a bottle of maple syrup, then took an enormous bite and chewed noisily, staring straight ahead. Linda watched Anna, her mouth tight.

Megan cleared her throat. "What are we doing this morning?" she asked Linda politely.

"Mm?" Linda asked, looking over at Megan. "Oh, Thomas needs you girls to deliver a load of corn to a farmer on the other side of town. You should be back by afternoon."

Megan slid two pancakes onto her plate. They were works of art, fluffy and golden, and studded with huge blueberries. Sarah reached over Megan's shoulder and forked three slices of bacon beside the pancakes.

Thomas came in and washed his hands at the sink. They were crusted with dirt. "Linda, I'm going to make a change in the morning's schedule," he told her, wiping his hands on a red-striped dishtowel. "I'm going to send one of the boys with Megan to Coothy's. Anna can stay back and help us paint the upstairs hallway." He smiled at his niece. "I've barely gotten a chance to talk with you since you got here. This way we can visit."

"Cool," Anna replied. She emptied half a mug of coffee in one gulp. "I hope you don't mind that I'm a really bad painter."

"You can do the rolling." Thomas sat down at the table with his own coffee, just as the screen door opened and the boys tramped in, in various stages of alertness. Megan saw Anna immediately straighten at the sight of Jordan.

The boys distributed themselves around the table and immediately began shoveling in pancakes. Within minutes, the platter was empty and Sarah was rushing to pour more batter on the griddle. "Hey, are you guys excited about the campfire tonight?" she asked, leaning against the stove as she waited for the pancakes to crisp.

"What campfire?" Robert asked, rubbing his eyes. "Sounds like fun."

"Thursday night tradition," Sarah said. "Just for us younguns—Thomas and Linda don't come. We all go up to this fantastic bonfire place back in the woods and play music, hang out, that sort of thing. Tonight at nine."

"Great," Jordan said. "Isaac has a guitar. I didn't bring mine."

"That's okay," Sarah said. "Dave's bringing his mandolin, so you can try that out, if you want."

Thomas started talking about the plans for the day. "I think I'll send Jordan with you, Megan, so Robert can help Dave," he said. "It shouldn't be a long outing. You'll just drive out, unload where he wants, and then come on back."

No one stopped talking or eating, but Megan felt as if a silence had fallen over the room. She focused on her pancakes, which sat in a pool of syrup. Three hours alone with Jordan. She felt exceedingly aware of Anna on her left, as if her skin had suddenly sprouted antennae. Megan swallowed the lump of pancake in her throat and hesitantly raised her eyes. Jordan gave her an easy smile. Anna was staring fixedly at her own sticky plate.

After the breakfast dishes were stacked in the sink, Anna trailed Megan out onto the porch, while Jordan went up to the tractor shed to retrieve the truck. Megan bent over, fiddling with her ankle socks and tying and retying her shoe. Anything to keep from seeing Anna's face. Megan felt like she'd done something wrong, though she knew she hadn't. At last she straightened up.

Anna's face sagged and her mouth was turned down. "I can't believe I'm not going." She sank down slowly onto a wicker chair nearby.

"Come on, we're delivering corn." Megan knelt down beside the chair. "Please, lighten up." There was a metallic taste in her mouth. Inside, she was dancing at the prospect of three hours alone with Jordan, but at the same time, hating herself for it. *It's just a few hours.*

Anna stared directly into Megan's face, as if she could see into her mind. "And *you* get to go."

Then the truck rumbled up to the porch, loaded with sacks of corn, and Jordan waved cheerfully. "Come on!" he called, and beeped the horn. Megan stood, brushing grit from her knees.

"See you this afternoon, okay?" she said.

Anna said nothing. Megan waved as they drove off, but her friend just sat as if propped in her chair. Megan watched her in the rearview mirror until the truck rounded a bend in the driveway and Anna was hidden from view.

Megan and Jordan were quiet as they pulled out onto the road toward the little town. The cab of the truck felt very small and enclosed. Megan was keenly aware of the foot of ripped gray seat in between the two of them. *Why doesn't someone say something?* She put her hands in her lap, then crossed her arms over her chest. *Is this going to be an awkward disaster?* The weight of Anna pressed down on Megan heavily. It should be her in this truck. At the same time, just the sight of Jordan's tanned, broad hands on the steering wheel made her ears grow hot. Then she heard her own voice, as if from someone else.

"Do you know how to get where we're going?" she asked.

He spoke at the same time. "Isn't it great to get off the farm for a while?"

They laughed, and just like that, she felt the awkwardness vanish. Megan slid down in her seat and kicked off her sneakers, propping her feet on the dashboard. "Yes, to your question," she said.

"And yes to yours." Jordan stopped at a stop sign, then turned right past a modernist house that looked like a pile of blue and pink building blocks. "Thomas gave me directions before we left." He lifted himself off the seat slightly and dug in his back pocket, handing Megan a folded piece of paper. "Want to navigate?"

"Sure." Megan tried to decipher Thomas's scratchy writing. "Let's see. Left on Maple Knoll. Have you done that yet?"

"Yeah, we just did. We're on Main now. Town's straight ahead."

Megan snorted a little at the thought of town. It seemed like a long time ago that she'd stumbled off the bus.

Jordan looked over. "What?"

"Nothing." Megan shook her head. "It's just that it seems like I've been at the farm forever, you know? But it's only been four days. I remember that's how camp used to be when I was little. I only would go for a week, but somehow, that one week seemed as long as the whole school year."

They reached the outskirts of the tiny town. Then they passed J & B Pawn, the liquor store, and the pharmacy. The same guys were still sitting on their barrels near the garage. Megan wondered if they ever moved or were just rooted there, like trees.

Then town disappeared behind them, and farmland spread out on either side. Megan cranked her window down and leaned her head against the back of the seat, appreciating the hot breeze on her face. She felt so relaxed. It was a relief not to have to monitor Anna and worry about her.

No, that was disloyal. Anna was her best friend. *Push that thought away.*

"So, what did your parents think about you working on a farm all summer?" Jordan asked. He was driving with one hand at the bottom of the wheel, the other elbow cocked out the window. The sun shone through his thick hair. At the corners of his eyes, Megan could see faint white squint lines in his tanned face.

"My dad didn't really care what I did. I think my mom was glad I was getting out of Cleveland for a while. This last school year was kind of . . . difficult." Megan swallowed, thinking of herself sitting alone in the cafeteria. "They're not really the farm types, though. They're lawyers."

He nodded. "They probably wouldn't be too into the sheep, then, right?"

Megan laughed, thinking of her blond mother throwing hay

bales around. "Not too much. My mom's more of a cat person. How about your parents? What did they think about the farm job?"

Jordan shrugged. "They're big, big hippies, so to them, it was, like, why *wouldn't* I work on a farm? The only thing better in their mind would have been if I'd volunteered at a Buddhist retreat or something." He shook his head. "You should have heard them when I got that road crew job last summer. *Pollutes the environment, toxic chemicals, encourages dependency on cars,*" he mimicked. "You'd think I started working for the Republican Party."

"Hey, how do you know *I'm* not a Republican?" Megan teased. "You might've just insulted me."

Jordan grinned. "No, you can't be a Republican. You're way too cute."

Megan laughed just as they both realized they'd crossed some invisible line. They fell silent.

"I don't think it's too much farther—" Jordan started to say just as something under the hood gave a pop and the truck shuddered. They looked at each other.

"Is it supposed to smell like burning rubber?" Megan asked.

"I'm sure it's nothing big," Jordan assured her. He pulled over to the side of the road, bumping on the uneven gravel, then climbed out of the cab and opened the hood. Megan got out too. She tried to peer at the engine, but she was distracted by standing so close to Jordan. She could see the smooth, tanned skin at the back of his neck, broken only by the gleam of a thin silver chain he wore under his shirt.

"It could be the fan belt." Jordan pointed at what looked like a mass of unrelated rubber pieces and greasy metal cylinders. "See how it's getting frayed there?"

"Oh, sure," Megan agreed, pretending she could see it. "Do you think we should call Thomas?"

Jordan slammed the hood. "I think we'll be okay for this trip." He grinned at her confidently, and she couldn't help smiling back.

"I'm just going to trust you on this one."

"Good choice, because I know nothing about cars." He winked.

Back in the truck, Megan dug into a bag of food Sarah had handed her as they left. "I'm already starving." She pawed past a few apples and a bag of carrot sticks before pulling out a plastic container of pasta salad. She held it up. "You want some of this?" It looked amazing—fresh pasta with gleaming chunks of tomato, olives, and peppers, all seasoned with bright green basil from the farm garden.

Jordan nodded. "Yeah." He tilted his head toward Megan. "Right in there." He opened his mouth like a baby bird, and Megan held a fork up so he could eat off a few pieces. "Damn, that's good."

Megan tucked her legs up under her and ate a mouthful herself as Jordan swung the truck around a series of dog-leg turns, down into a valley. The farms were gone now and the trees crowded close to the road, their drooping branches hanging low. Megan held up another forkful of pasta. "So, do you *like* the farm work so far?" she asked.

Jordan nodded and accepted the bite. "Don't stab my face with that fork, okay?" he joked. "Yeah, I love it, actually. I want to major in sustainable agriculture in college, so this is the perfect summer job."

"Are you going to be a senior next year?"

He shook his head. "I just graduated. I'm going to OSU in the fall. I cannot *wait* to get out of Lodi. You have no idea." High rock walls rose up on either side of the road, dripping with moisture and streaked with moss.

Megan stuck the salad container back in the bag at her feet. "Hey, is this where we need to be?" She pointed to a brown and white ENTERING JOHN BEAN STATE PARK sign.

"No, shoot." Jordan did a U-turn in the middle of the narrow road. "We must have missed a turn." The truck climbed out of the valley, past the rock walls. They were really in more of a gorge, Megan realized, and there was no way a farm was going to be down here. She looked at the directions and realized that she'd misread "turn left after 8 miles" as "turn left after 3 miles."

They were nearing the top of the valley road when the engine made a popping sound again and the burning rubber smell grew stronger. Megan waited for the engine to sputter or die, but nothing happened except that Jordan started whistling a little tune.

She looked over at him. He was tapping his fingers on the wheel in time to his whistling.

"I smell burning rubber again," she pointed out.

He nodded. "Yeah, but see, if you pretend you can't smell it, it'll just go away." He gave Megan a big, toothy grin and she giggled.

"Okay, wow. What an amazing plan." She closed her eyes for a minute and pretended to concentrate. Then she opened them. "Wow, that really worked!" The rubber smell was stronger than ever. "I can't smell even a bit of rubber."

Jordan grinned. "See?"

"I knew you were brilliant," Megan teased. She pointed as they approached a stop sign. "This is probably the turn." There were more farms again. "There it is." A rough white sign splattered with mud was stuck in the ground on a patch of unmowed grass. BARKER FARM: HISTORIC FARMLAND FOR SALE it read.

Jordan turned onto the narrow, muddy driveway and swerved around a series of potholes. Around a bend, the farmhouse loomed before them, tall, gaunt, and cheerless. The shutters were falling off the white house, and some of the louvers lay on the grass. Jordan glanced over at Megan and made a noise like a ghost. Megan giggled a little nervously.

They parked by a large, rambling barn. The place was still, except for a distant barking dog. "Hello?" Megan called out.

"Got my corn?" A harsh voice came from behind them, and they both whirled around. A man looking straight out of the painting *American Gothic*, right down to the deep lines carved into his face, stood in the entrance to the barn, holding a shovel.

"Yep, we've got it." Megan tried to sound friendly and cheerful. "Are you Mr."—she squinted at her paper—"Cootie?"

The lines in his face deepened. "Coothy."

"Sorry about that. It's nice to meet you."

"The corn's in the truck. We're happy to help you unload it," Jordan said.

"Come here," Coothy ordered, turning away. Megan and Jordan glanced at each other and followed him through the wet, knee-high weeds to the back of the barn. "Up there." He pointed to a small shed at the top of a long slope. It looked very far away. "Corn goes up in there." Then the man turned and went back into the barn. After a minute, they heard the scrape of a shovel.

Jordan leaned over. "You think he's burying a body in there?" he murmured.

Megan laughed in spite of herself. "How are we going to carry those bags up there?" They walked over to the slope, which was slick with mud. The shed had to be at least a quarter mile up. "The guy's insane!"

"Yeah, he's a nut job," Jordan agreed. "But don't worry, I've got this one." He turned and walked back to the barn. At the door, he stopped and called in. "Mr. Coothy?"

The farmer appeared out of the gloom. "What?"

Jordan smiled easily, as if he were about to invite his favorite nephew to play catch in the yard. "We're happy to help you with the corn, but we're going to need a wheelbarrow."

"Wheelbarrow's broken," Coothy grunted. "Just carry them up."

"Well, I'm afraid that's kind of far up," Jordan said calmly.

Coothy said nothing.

"Okay," Jordan finally said. "We'll just stack the corn somewhere dry, and we'll be happy to come back later, once your wheelbarrow's fixed."

Coothy opened and closed his mouth a few times. Megan guessed he wasn't used to having people refuse his orders. Jordan didn't wait for a response. Instead, he walked back to the truck and began dragging out the bags of corn and piling them neatly on the porch, against the wall of the house, where they would be protected. Megan hurried over and helped him stack the bags. All the while, Coothy still hadn't moved from his place in the barn doorway.

"That guy's going to stab us with a pitchfork or something," Megan hissed, hefting one end of her bag.

Jordan just smiled. "Nah. There were a ton of guys like him on the road crew. They just got off on ordering everyone around. It was a big power trip for them. Seriously, what are we going to do? Break our backs hauling that stuff up that hill? We'd be here forever!"

After they'd finished dragging the bags onto the porch, Megan expected they'd get right back into the truck. But Jordan walked back over to the barn. Coothy had disappeared again.

"Jordan, stop!" Megan stage-whispered. "What are you doing?"

He paused at the barn entrance and called out cheerfully, "Everything's unloaded, Mr. Coothy. Thanks—we're going to get going." There was only silence. "Hope you have a good day."

Megan almost sprinted to the truck, collapsing in the seat. She raised her head as Jordan climbed in beside her. "You're lucky we didn't get shot. It would've been your fault."

Jordan grinned and twisted the key in the ignition. "I could've taken him." He drove back down the muddy driveway and out onto the blacktop. Even the sunshine seemed brighter now that they were off that farm. Megan glanced at the dashboard clock. "Noon. That's not too bad."

Jordan stretched first one arm and then another over his head. "I know, right? Dave said they were grilling tonight for dinner too. I wouldn't want to miss that." He swung the truck around another curve. There were no farms on this stretch. The road sat low down, with high, rocky embankments rising up on either side. Almost above their heads stretched rough rail fences. Thorny wild-rose bushes hung down thickly, their simple white flowers gazing out at the roadside.

"That was great, the way you handled that guy," Megan said.

He waved his hand in dismissal.

"No, seriously," Megan insisted. "I mean, you didn't argue with him. You just told him what we were doing and then did it. I'd never be able to stand up to someone like that."

Jordan hesitated. "I've noticed that's hard for you, isn't it? Standing up to people?" He didn't say "Anna," but Megan knew that's what he meant. She started to feel embarrassed that he'd noticed Anna pushing her around, but when he looked over at her, his face held nothing but understanding. The embarrassment flowed away.

"Yeah," she just said softly.

The gears ground as Jordan urged the truck up the hilly road. The rubber smell was stronger than before. Jordan threw Megan a look like, "Don't say it." She smiled back and bit her lip, gazing ostentatiously out the window.

A popping noise came from under the hood, and the engine noise grew louder. The truck started to shake.

"Whooaa." Megan gripped the side of her door. The steering wheel looked like it was trying to rip itself out of Jordan's hands. Megan glanced at the dashboard again. The needle on the temperature gauge was all the way over to the right. Megan couldn't read the numbers from where she was sitting, but she could see the colors, and she figured that red probably meant "hot." *Do engines ever explode?* she thought nervously.

The shaking grew more violent. "Hang on!" Jordan said. He managed to guide the truck over to the side of the road just before the engine died.

They both sat frozen for a moment, Jordan still gripping the wheel. Off to her right, Megan heard a bird chirping loudly in a rosebush. *Dreeep. Dreeep.* If she closed her eyes, she could almost imagine they'd pulled over to stretch their legs.

Jordan opened the door and went around to the front. He held his palm an inch above the hood, then called to Megan. "Hey, is there a rag or something in there?"

Megan searched around and found a torn towel stuffed behind one of the seats. She climbed out and handed it to him. "What's up?"

Using the towel like a pot holder, Jordan gingerly popped the latch and opened the hood. "Ah! Jeez, the engine's superhot. See, the fan belt broke." He pointed, and Megan peered in at the wide, flat loop of rubber that now hung limply, the two ends shredded. "Without a fan belt, the radiator overheats in, like, one second." He sighed and released the propstick, letting the hood bang down.

Megan's shoulders sagged. "So basically, we're screwed." She looked both ways on the road. There wasn't a single sign of life, unless you counted a robin pecking enthusiastically on the berm. Also, she recalled with increasingly sinking spirits, not a single car had passed them the whole time they'd been pulled over. "What are we going to do?" she almost wailed. Visions of herself and Jordan lying by the truck starved to death and picked at by vultures swam through her mind.

Jordan put his arm over her shoulders. He felt very solid and very warm, Megan noticed even through her distress. And very nice.

"Hey, what're you getting all upset for?" he asked. "Have you forgotten what century you're living in?" He pulled out his cell phone, and Megan sighed with relief.

"Duh," she said. "I feel stupid."

He thumbed his phone. "Not at all. We'll call Thomas and have him come out. . . ." He trailed off, staring down at the phone.

"What?" Megan asked, but even before the word was out of her mouth, she knew.

"No service," they both said at the same time.

They looked at each other. Megan dug her own phone from her pocket. Zero bars. She held it up and waved it around in the air, as if that might help. Still zero bars.

"Well, should we start walking?"

Megan looked around at the deserted road. "Back to Coothy's?"

Jordan steered her along the side of the blacktop to the right. "I'm not sure he'd be thrilled to see us. Besides, it's almost six miles back." He started walking briskly. "It's not like we're in the middle of the desert. We'll just knock at the nearest house and ask to use their phone."

Megan trotted by his side. At least she'd worn her trail sneakers. "Let me ask you something," she said after a minute. "Are you *ever* in a bad mood?"

"I don't know, why? Do I seem unnaturally happy or something?" He reached out and plucked a rose from a nearby bramble and twirled it between his fingers as they walked.

"Well, not happy, exactly." The road was steeper now, and Megan tried not to pant as they walked. "Just . . . I don't know. You don't get rattled." But as she spoke, she remembered his embarrassment when she'd found Anna and him in the stall before Sweetie's birth. She smiled to herself. Maybe he wasn't quite as unshakable as he seemed.

Jordan caught her look. "What? Why're you smiling like that?" He reached over and gently tucked the little rose behind Megan's ear. His fingers brushed her cheek, and she swallowed. Her cheek burned where he'd touched it.

"Hey, there's a house," she fumbled, not quite ready to figure out just what that moment meant. She pointed to a small brick bungalow atop a gentle rise. A large American flag fluttered from a pole in the center of the lawn.

They walked a little faster. The sweat trickled down the side of her temple. Very attractive. They neared the driveway. The flagpole was surrounded by a ring of pink geraniums, the front walk spotless and the grass edged as if with a ruler. The front door was shut, but a large, shiny truck sat in the driveway.

As she followed Jordan up the front walk, Megan fingered the flower behind her ear. Was he flirting with her? Was that right, since he was with Anna? *But are they officially together, Megan?* the voice in her head asked. *Isn't it Anna who likes* him?

Megan pictured herself cradling Jordan's hand against her cheek. And then him putting his arms around her waist and pulling her against him. . . . Megan shook her head and blinked hard. They were standing at the front door. The image had been so strong that, for an instant, it had blotted out anything else.

Jordan pressed the bell and they waited, staring at a small wooden plaque on the front door that read EAST, WEST, HOME'S BEST. The words were surrounded by a pattern of apples. A few minutes later, the door was opened by a pleasant-faced blond woman.

"Yes?"

"Hi, I'm Jordan and this is Megan. We work for Thomas Neale at Given Farm." Jordan smiled confidently, and Megan tried to look sweet and harmless. "Our truck broke down about a half mile back, and we can't get any cell coverage. Do you think we could use your phone to call our boss?"

The woman looked doubtful for a moment, and Megan didn't blame her. It sounded like the perfect setup for a robbery in a movie or something. But people must be more trusting out in the country, because the woman stepped back and held open the door. "Come on in. The phone's in the kitchen."

They stepped into the cool hall. The house smelled of lemon Pledge and old furniture. Megan caught a glimpse of a huge sectional sofa and a TV on mute.

In the yellow-tiled kitchen, the woman pointed to a phone on the wall. "There you go." She hesitated as Jordan lifted the receiver. "Are you two hungry?" she asked.

Megan's stomach gave a hollow rumble. They'd eaten the pasta salad a long time ago, and who knew when they'd make it back to the farm? "Oh, no, we're okay," Megan said politely.

But the woman was already pulling open the refrigerator door and taking out bologna, lettuce, and bread. Megan shifted on her feet.

Across the room, Jordan was nodding his head and twisting the phone cord around his wrist. "Okay, okay. Got it." He looked around, then grabbed a pen from the counter and wrote a number on the back of his hand.

"I'm sorry," Megan said apologetically. "May I use your bathroom?"

"Oh, sure." The woman pointed to a door with a mayonnaise-smeared knife.

When Megan returned, Jordan was sitting at the kitchen island with his arms on the counter, talking to the woman as if he'd known her for years. She smiled and nodded as she wrapped two bologna sandwiches in foil.

"Meg," Jordan said as she came in. She did not fail to notice the nickname, but she couldn't—or wouldn't—dwell on its meaning right now. "Thomas said to call for a tow, but the driver said he doesn't know when he can get here. We're supposed to wait by the truck. Sarah's selling at the farmers' market all day, so the guy'll drop us there and we can catch a ride home with her."

The nice lady stuck the sandwiches in a grocery bag, along with two bottles of water. "This will keep you while you wait," she said. "I've never known a tow truck to take less than two hours."

"Thank you so, so much." Megan gratefully accepted the sack of sandwiches, and they walked toward the door. The woman waved at them from the porch as they headed back down the driveway.

The sun was not quite as fierce overhead now, the sky broken up by a few fluffy white clouds. Without saying anything, Jordan took the sandwiches from Megan's hand and swung the bag as they walked. Even that little gesture seemed sweet and gentlemanly.

They didn't say anything for a long moment, but the silence didn't feel awkward. Then Jordan pointed down. "Look."

They were walking in stride together. Right, left, right, left, perfectly matched. She laughed up at Jordan. "That wasn't even on purpose."

"See, this makes it even easier." He slid his arm around her shoulders and pulled her against him as they walked. His hand was firm against her upper arm. Megan's heart gave a thud and she stumbled, almost toppling into the drainage ditch on the side of the road.

"Whoops!" Jordan caught at her arm.

"Thanks," she managed, trying to catch her breath. For a moment, they stood facing each other, very close. No guy had ever, *ever* looked at her this way before. His eyes dropped to her lips. Megan thought her heart was going to pound its way out of her chest.

"Um, so, should we keep going?" she stammered, breaking his gaze. *God, my hands are dripping sweat.* She wiped them surreptitiously on her jeans.

"What?" Jordan didn't seem to hear her at first. "Oh, yeah. We should." He sighed.

A few minutes down the road, Jordan stopped. "Hey!"

Fat, red raspberries hung off several bushes by the road. Megan looked at Jordan and grinned. "Dessert," she said. He nodded and pulled the sandwiches out of the bag. They quickly started picking into the grocery sack. In only a few minutes, the bag was half full of juicy, syrupy-smelling berries.

Back at the truck, they settled down on the shoulder, away from any traffic, though this had to be the loneliest country road Megan had ever seen.

Megan unwrapped her sandwich, and they chewed companionably for a minute.

"You're a good person to get stranded with, Meg," Jordan said, swallowing.

There it was again. Her nickname fell like a caress on her ears. "Thanks." She tried to pry a layer of bread off the roof of her mouth. "You are too. Like I said before, you don't seem fazed by very much." She opened one of the water bottles and took a long, cool swig.

He shrugged. "I don't know. It's probably from how I grew up." He finished one half of his sandwich and started on the other.

Megan waited for him to go on, but Jordan dug into the bag of berries and popped several into his mouth one by one.

"How come?" she finally prompted. She ate a couple of berries too. The juice stained her fingers, but the taste was intense on her tongue.

Jordan stretched his legs out in front of him on the grass. He looked over at Megan. "It's weird, I guess I feel like you'll understand this."

Megan nodded. "I want to."

"I grew up in a little town, and I had kind of a hard time."

"How so?" Megan looked at him. It was hard for her to imagine anyone as gorgeous as he was having a hard time. A little breeze brushed her cheek and she raised her face to it.

"My parents were big back-to-the-land hippies." He smiled, but not a happy smile. "They moved to Lodi when I was six to get closer to nature—that's the way they always put it. They built a log cabin for us to live in. Lodi is this little town where nothing had changed since the 1950s, and they showed up and ran around talking about the Earth Mother and living in a 'more human space' and just expected that everyone would love them as much as they loved each other."

Megan sensed he was waiting for her to laugh at him, but she didn't feel like laughing. She could see that he was sensitive about this topic. She raked the grass with her fingers and waited for him to go on.

After a moment, he did. "There was always this sense from our parents that we were better than everyone else. When I was little, I actually believed it. But when I got to be eight or so, I didn't want to eat carrot soup and wear shirts my mom wove. I wanted pizza and a Raiders jersey, you know? Of course, they'd *never* get me or my older sister anything like that, and all the kids in town knew it." He clasped his arms around his updrawn knees. "We were basically the freaks of the town." He gave a little, humorless laugh. "Thanks, Mom and Dad."

Without thinking, she reached out and put her hand over his. "That sounds really hard."

He shrugged. "It got a little better when I was older. I learned how to let things roll off my back."

"Are your parents still in Lodi?"

Jordan pushed the food trash aside and lay back on the dry grass. "Yeah, they're still there. And still self-righteous."

"I used to get teased a bunch when I was younger," Megan offered.

"You?" Jordan raised his head a little to look at her. "No, seriously?"

"I'm glad it's that hard to believe. It doesn't seem so crazy to me. I had no idea how to dress, for one thing." She looked down at her T-shirt, which now sported several berry stains. "I still don't, actually."

"That's not true." Jordan smiled up at her from the golden

grass. "I think you dress cute. Here, look at these clouds." Jordan pointed up. "You have to lie down to see them."

With a feeling that she was taking another step into dangerous territory, Megan eased herself flat on her back beside him and stared up at the pale blue sky. Delicate cirrus clouds like fish scales trailed off to the horizon.

They turned to look at each other at the same time. Their faces were only a few inches apart. Megan could see the blond stubble on his chin and felt the electrifying tingle of his bare arm against hers. Her heart thudded. His eyes flitted to her hair, then her mouth. Megan felt herself trembling. For an overwhelming instant, he moved closer, and she quickly looked back at the sky.

Jordan cleared his throat. "So, why'd it stop?"

"Wh-what?" She closed her eyes, trying to recover.

"The teasing. You said you used to get teased."

"Oh, that." She managed to stop trembling and took a deep breath. "Well, I had Anna. She was like my savior. She had a thousand and one friends and I couldn't figure out why she had chosen *me* above everyone else, but she did. No one would ever tease me when Anna was nearby."

"And so you feel like you owe her."

A swallow swooped above them. The sun was stronger now, sending powerful midafternoon rays across the fields.

Megan shook her head and propped herself up on her elbows. "I'm sorry, what?"

"You feel like you owe her," Jordan repeated. "You know, for rescuing you. That's why you let her take shots at you, isn't it?"

"Anna doesn't take shots at me," Megan replied automatically, but she knew that Jordan had put into words what she'd always felt but never could say. Anna *did* push her around, and Megan knew she didn't usually stand up for herself. Instead, she just got that hot, angry, shameful feeling whenever Anna poked her with a little verbal jab. Or things like driving past her in town. Anna was always doing that stuff—and she had ever since they were little. But it had gotten worse since Mike.

"It's not like that," she tried to explain. But she dropped her eyes under his steady gaze, feeling an unexpected flush of shame. It was as if he'd seen into some secret part of herself that she'd always thought was invisible to other people.

Then she felt his hand on hers. "What I'm trying to say is that I think we're more alike than you realize." He looked into her eyes again. "I think we've both spent a lot of time hiding." He leaned toward her.

For a moment, she stopped breathing. *No. No. No! Do not kiss him. Do not. Never again, never again. You will lose her forever, Megan! She is your best friend—almost your only friend. Remember Mike. Remember Mike.* Megan shook her head as if to knock some sense back into it. "Look," she said, "what's, um, what's the deal with you and Anna?" Her heart pounded madly, but it needed to be asked. They couldn't keep going on like this.

Jordan sighed, as if he'd been expecting the question. "I don't know, honestly." He spread his hands. "At first, yeah, she seemed like a fun girl, and we flirted around plenty before the rest of you arrived. But that was it. I never kissed her or said anything to make her think we were, like, together." He shook his head. "But lately, it seems like she's gotten kind of . . . intense, you know?"

Megan nodded. She did know.

Jordan looked her full in the face. "I never led her on. I want you to know that. I'm not a jerk like that."

"I know," Megan almost-whispered. She felt him take her hand and slowly entwine his fingers with hers. She couldn't take her eyes from his face. Then he leaned toward her, tilting his head, and she felt her lips part slightly. *No!*

With all the will in her body, Megan leapt to her feet and walked a few yards away, gazing down the road. "The truck's really late. He'd better get here before the mosquitoes come out."

Jordan didn't say anything, and Megan turned around, her face full of the struggle inside her. *Please understand. I can't do this to her.* In response, he rose to his feet and went to stand next to her. He nodded and, with one finger, brushed her lips briefly, his touch glowing like the flare of a match. "Yeah, I know."

CHAPTER 8

The farmers' market was nestled in a charming little shopping district in the midst of Ault Hill. As they alighted from the rumbling tow truck and waved good-bye to the driver, Megan looked around at the little white tents selling riding clothes and cashmere sweaters and wondered how this place could exist so close to the world of J & B Pawn.

Given Farm's stall was set up about halfway down the row of vendors. She could see Sarah standing over a basket of green peppers, talking to a middle-aged guy in a golf shirt. Then, with a shiver, she saw Anna and Robert.

Jordan hadn't said they would be here. She knew she hadn't *technically* done anything wrong, but shame and guilt still rose hot in her throat as she approached. She didn't dare look at Jordan.

"Hey there!" Sarah greeted them cheerfully from behind the wooden plank that served as their counter. "Thomas told us about the truck—that sucks. Glad you guys got back okay."

"You find the corn guy?" Robert asked as he stacked empty berry boxes.

"Yeah, we found him all right." Megan slipped behind the counter, and Jordan started helping load the strawberry trays into the van parked behind the stall.

Megan rearranged the tomatoes into a pyramid before daring to cast her eyes over to Anna. Her friend was counting money into a cash box and didn't look up. Of course she was concentrating, but Megan thought she saw a whiteness around Anna's pursed lips.

Megan was about to say something when a girl with a peasant skirt and two young guys with bushy beards approached the booth. They were all wearing T-shirts that read AULT HILL FARMERS' MARKET. They reminded Megan of a cross between nineteenth-century homesteaders and hippies. It wasn't a look that she was used to in suburban Cleveland, but out here it seemed to work.

"How're you guys?" the girl asked.

"Hey!" Sarah kissed each on the cheek, then turned to the others. "This is Dee, Murray, and Charles. They're in charge of the farmers' market association."

Megan nodded.

"Your tomatoes look fantastic," Dee said. She picked up one of the plump, juicy globes and hefted it in her palm. "Beautiful. How many acres did you guys plant?"

"Just one. You know, we fertilized this year with cow manure instead of horse, and I really think it's making a difference." Sarah smiled at a young woman with a double stroller who had stopped to look at the piles of parsley and basil. "Hey, are you guys coming to Midsummer Night this year?"

"Oh, definitely," one of the guys said. Megan couldn't remember if he was Charles or Murray. "Wouldn't miss it."

"Thomas throws a big party around the solstice every year," Sarah explained to the others. "It's Saturday night out on the lawn. It's great—we cook, and there's an old-timey band. Everyone gets dressed up."

"That sounds like fun," Megan said.

"See you guys then," Dee said. She waved, and the three strolled away down the aisle of stalls. There was a last-minute rash of people buying things, and for fifteen minutes or so, Megan was too busy to even look up.

Finally, there was a lull, and Megan sank down in one of the lawn chairs behind the table. Sarah perched beside her. "So, how was the trip? Did you meet Coothy?"

"Oh my God." Megan laughed. "He is unbelievable. Well, I mean, the whole trip was kind of a disaster from the start." She started telling Sarah about the wrong turn and the engine noises. "Then, at the farm, this guy looked like something from an old horror flick. He never let go of this old shovel." She mimed Coothy's grumpy stance while Sarah and Robert laughed.

"So, he says his wheelbarrow's broken and he actually wants

us to carry the corn up this insane hill," Jordan said. "And *Megan* told him that we absolutely wouldn't—"

"You're such a liar!" Megan laughed at him. "I spent the whole time trying to hide behind you! If I could drive a stick, I would've left you to deal with him."

Jordan widened his eyes mockingly. "No, seriously! You guys should've seen her, she was so tough—"

Megan shoved his shoulder. "Shut up! He's so wrong, you guys. . . ." They grinned at each other. Sarah and Robert were laughing too, but Anna'd stopped counting the money, and her face made Megan's hands grow cold and her mouth go dry.

Anna wasn't laughing. She was still, as if every muscle in her body had frozen. Her eyes rested on Megan, glittering and hard.

Megan saw the accusation on her face, and her insides shriveled. Jordan didn't notice—he was describing the truck breaking down. Megan forced a smile.

Anna didn't respond. Instead, she took a berry from the box in front of her and bit into it, chewing slowly and deliberately, never taking her eyes from Megan's face.

The sky was streaked with purple over the fields as the sun set in a liquid blaze, but in the woods, it was already dark. Megan stumbled over a root sticking out of the crude path and lurched against Anna, who grabbed her so she wouldn't fall, her flashlight swinging against the trees. They both giggled nervously because of the dark. Whatever tension had surfaced that afternoon had faded, and Anna seemed like her old self again.

They were last in the line that snaked through the hilly woods. Dave was in front, carrying a mandolin, followed by Sarah, who had a bag of cookies. Isaac had brought his guitar, and Robert and Jordan both carried wood on their backs in canvas slings.

"This is going to be so fun," Anna burbled beside Megan. "I love bonfires, don't you?" She was practically skipping along the path, despite the rough footing.

"Hey, I love bonfires too," Robert declared, clearly aiming his comment at Anna. "We should've brought stuff for s'mores. I haven't had those since I went to camp."

He's trying—no one can say he's not, Megan thought. She had to admire the guy's persistence.

"Uh-huh," Anna murmured dismissively and walked faster to catch up with Jordan.

Don't, Megan thought instinctively as she hurried after her friend. But of course, she couldn't say that.

Luckily, they started up a steep incline, and Anna was forced to slow down before she could reach Jordan. Megan trudged along, feeling the pull in her calves. They were climbing a sort of ridge that traced the edge of a deep ravine. The trees were thick and the path was a switchback, winding around the trunks.

Megan strained her eyes, hoping to see the top, but the darkness was complete now, and all she could see were the beams of several flashlights.

"Not much farther," Dave called back through the line.

Not long after, they emerged from the woods at the ridge's

peak to find a clearing with a large charred spot ringed with stones. Larger rocks and a few big logs formed the seats around the campfire area. There was a general sigh of relief as everyone put down their various parcels. Robert and Jordan thumped their load of firewood to the ground, and Jordan knelt to undo the bindings. Dave propped his mandolin against a rock and immediately started scraping dirt and random leaves away from the fire circle, while Sarah started taking the cookies and a big bag of marshmallows from her sack.

"This is awesome!" Robert declared, surveying the scene. His voice was loud but oddly flat in the night air. Megan agreed silently. The darkness was a little thinner up here, now that they were out of the dense woods. The night breeze fluttered by her face, smelling of damp leaves and quiet, secret places.

Jordan looked up from untying the wood and caught her eye. He smiled at her and she smiled back, suddenly overcome by the memory of his face so close to hers this afternoon. Furtively, she glanced at Anna, who was kneeling, picking something out of her shoe. She hadn't seen them. Megan felt a brief flash of relief.

"Hey, guys. Find some kindling, okay?" Dave said.

Everyone scattered to pick up sticks. Megan wandered off to a nearby pine tree and aimed her flashlight at the ground, then set it down. She knelt and started swiping together handfuls of dry pine needles. Those seemed good for starting a fire. She shuffled a few feet farther to reach for more. The others were on the opposite side of the fire ring, their voices faint. The only sound, besides her breath in her ears, was the crackle of needles beneath her knees.

Megan slowly scraped together a big pile, thinking of the way Jordan's eyes flashed so blue in the sun. Just like glacier ice.

Something grabbed her ankle. Megan shrieked and her hand jerked, scattering her pile.

"Hah! Gotcha!" Anna chortled.

Megan took a deep breath, trying to calm her heart. Her knees ached with the adrenaline that had shot through her system.

"You really freaked me out," she said. "I didn't even hear you." She paused. "What were you doing sneaking up on me?"

Anna grinned. "I was finding wood. Duh." Her hands were empty.

Megan swallowed. "Oh." Something about Anna's tone was off, though she couldn't quite put her finger on it.

Anna bent down and swiped up a twig. "Here, got some."

Back behind them, flames flared orange in the darkness. "Looks like they got the fire going without us," Megan said uneasily.

"Yeah, come on."

They walked back together and Anna took Megan's hand, swinging it as if they were girls on the playground again.

The fire glowed like a friendly beacon as Megan lowered herself onto a log. The flames in the center sent up showers of spark as they burned through sap in the twigs. She thought back to the summers she went to Camp Kern. They'd had a campfire every night, and ever since then, the smell of woodsmoke always drew up feelings of melancholy.

Strumming his guitar thoughtfully, Isaac was sunken into the shadows on the far side of the fire. He looked every inch the brooding musician. Nearby, Anna pressed close to Jordan's side, the length of her thigh against his. She studiously ignored Robert, who had seated himself on a rock beside her and was sending her wistful glances. Instead, she picked up Jordan's hand, entwining it with hers.

Megan swallowed and looked at her hands, which were grubby with dirt, then at the ground. *She* wanted to be the one sitting beside Jordan, holding his hand in a casual, proprietary way. Megan felt her stomach twist miserably.

Dave plucked at his mandolin, starting a folk song. After a few practice chords, Isaac joined in. Dave sang the lyrics in a surprisingly beautiful baritone. The song was about a bird-woman who drank from a mountain stream. Robert and Sarah sang the chorus, their voices blending with the pop and snap of the fire and the whispering rush of the wind through the treetops.

Sarah passed her the cookies. Megan shook her head. She didn't think she could eat anything with her stomach in knots.

"It's fun, isn't it, all of us hanging out?" Sarah asked kindly. She must have sensed Megan's misery.

Megan made herself nod. "Oh, definitely!" Her voice sounded false even to herself.

The cookies made a second round, and the marshmallows were about halfway gone. The fire had died to a low glow, and Dave reached back to throw another branch on. He came up with his hands empty.

"We're all out of wood," he said. "Let's get a few more branches, and we can hang out a little longer."

Everyone rose, a little stiffly, reluctant to leave the fading warmth. The night air had cooled since they sat down, and the dropping temperature was more pronounced as Megan wandered away from the fire. Her sneakers made no noise on the dry leaves. Quickly, she lost sight of the others as they scattered. Her flashlight was lying by her seat on the log, but it seemed too much trouble to go back for it.

Anna was nowhere to be seen. Megan assumed she'd followed Jordan. Good. At least she wasn't going to get pranked again. Someone crunched only a few feet away, but so hidden by the shadows she couldn't tell who it was. Idly, she bent down to retrieve a stick that was about the right size when suddenly, arms circled her waist, dragging her behind a thick tree trunk. Megan gasped, about to cry out, until she caught the whiff of cedar soap and realized it was Jordan.

He didn't speak, just turned her around and pulled her against him. He bent his head, pressing his mouth to hers. His lips were hot and smooth, and Megan leaned into him, still trying to catch her breath. He kissed her, and she kissed him back, thinking about nothing but the sensation of his arms around her body, his mouth on hers again and again. Then someone passed by in the dark—so close that Megan could almost reach out and touch her sleeve. It was Anna.

"Dave, there's a big branch over here," she called.

Instantly, they broke apart. Megan struggled to control her breathing. She looked up into Jordan's face, which was almost all shadow. A blossom of delight unfurled in her chest, sending delicious tendrils shooting to her fingers and toes. She knew he was feeling the same intensity she was—the kiss left no doubt. At the same time, Megan knew, without a doubt, that she had finally plummeted over the cliff she'd been edging toward since that first day in the kitchen.

CHAPTER 9

Megan stared sightlessly at the pages of the Somerset Maugham novel, which she held in front of her face like a shield. All she could think about was Jordan. His hands seemed to have seared Megan's flesh everywhere he had touched—her waist, her arms, the back of her neck. Her lips still burned.

"I think I really connected with Jordan tonight," Anna said from across the room.

Megan's fingers tightened on her book. "Hmm?" She peeked over the edge of the pages.

Anna was sitting on her bed, one leg drawn up under her chin as she carefully painted her toenails teal. Anna dipped the brush into the little bottle. "Well, for one thing, did you see him holding my hand?"

Megan thought of Anna caressing Jordan's fingers. "Sort of . . . ," she said slowly. She turned a page, keeping her face hidden, thinking of the Kafka story she'd read where the prisoner is punished by having a machine write the name of his crime on his skin, over and over again. She shuddered and resisted the urge to twist to look at Jordan in the farmhand photo, which she'd pinned over her bed.

"It was so good," Anna went on. "And he was, like, rubbing up against my thigh the whole time we were sitting there. I mean, it was getting embarrassing!" Her face was shining, and Megan could see that she didn't think it was embarrassing at all. Anna just liked saying that it was.

Swallowing hard, Megan sat up suddenly and grabbed her towel from the hook by the door. "I'm going to wash up." She clattered down the stairs without looking back.

Outside, the humid air seemed to press in on her, like a wet cloth draped over her face. Megan turned the faucet and watched the water swirl into the drain. The sulfur smell was strong in her nostrils.

"What's that?" Anna's voice came from behind her.

Megan jumped, and whirled around, clutching the narrow edge of the sink behind her. "What?" she fairly gasped.

"That." Anna swooped down to pick up a piece of folded paper lying on the ground.

"Oh, it's mine." Megan snatched it up first. "My training notes for Sweetie." The words seemed to fly from her mouth unbidden. She slid the paper into the pocket of her shorts. It must have fallen out, though she hadn't put it there. It had to be from Jordan. Megan felt alert like a rabbit, her eyes wide, trying to look in every direction at one time.

Anna draped her own towel over a nail and ran some water from the other faucet. "You look weird," she said, squeezing toothpaste onto her brush.

Megan buried her face in soapy lather. "I—I do feel a little sick." That wasn't a lie, at least. "Too many marshmallows."

Anna stuck her toothbrush in her mouth.

Megan rinsed her face fast and headed toward the cabin.

"Aren't you going to brush your teeth?" Anna called after her.

"I already did," Megan lied.

Inside, she quickly unfolded the note. Tilting the paper toward the dim lantern light, she read,

> Megan—I can't stop thinking about you.
> This afternoon by the truck was amazing.
> I wanted to kiss you then but I didn't,
> for reasons we both know. I hope you're
> not mad about tonight. We have to talk. J.

Megan's cheeks were flaming. Jordan must have slipped it into her pocket just after he kissed her.

Outside, the water shut off. *Fast, fast, get rid of it fast,* Megan thought. Then there were footsteps up the stairs. She looked around the cabin wildly. Footsteps across the porch. Megan reached over the edge of the bed and shoved the note under the mattress. Then, in one movement, she flopped over on her back and raised her book in front of her face. The screen door opened.

Megan stared at the yellowed page, trying not to breathe too loudly. Anna didn't speak. Then Megan heard her cross the room and the bed creak as she sat down. "You know, Meg," she said. "This is shaping up to be the best summer of my life."

The barn was cool in the early morning, and the only sound was the horses' peaceful munching of grain and hay. Megan rested her arms on the door of Rosie's stall, watching her eat while Sweetie nursed. She had lain awake, sweating under the sheet until the insect sounds had faded and the first birds sang from the trees. Then she had slipped out the door while Anna slept on.

Her head throbbed. Her eyes felt grainy, and she knew there were circles under them. She closed her eyes, and the sensation of Jordan's lips on hers, the scratch of his beard against her cheek, rushed at her. She gripped the edge of the stall door but forced her fingers to relax.

To distance herself, she dug into her pocket and pulled out her phone, thumbing through the missed calls. Her mother had tried to reach her three times yesterday, and Megan suspected that if she didn't call her back, the police would be showing up at Given Farm. Thomas probably wouldn't appreciate that.

Megan hit her home number and listened to the phone ring.

"Meg?" Her mother answered on the second ring. "Hi, honey!"

"Hi, Mom." Megan made sure her voice was both casual and happy. No indication of weird Anna vibes, no indication of kissing beautiful guys in the dark. No turmoil of anxiety, exhilaration, and misery. Just happy, upbeat, well-adjusted Megan.

"How do you like the farm?" Her mother asked eagerly.

Megan heard a rumbling voice in the background—her father, asking how she was.

"Oh, it's great!" Megan said. "Anna and I have a cabin to ourselves, and I get to train this new little foal." Sweetie was a safe subject.

Rosie finished her grain and ambled forward a few steps. Megan rubbed her nose, and then Sweetie pushed his way over.

"Sweetie's right here," Megan told her mother. "Here, he wants to say hi." She held the phone up to Sweetie's nose, and he snuffled at the screen with interest.

"Did you hear him?" Megan held the phone back to her own ear.

"Yes, he sounds lovely. Is Anna enjoying the farm too?" her mother asked.

Megan thought of Anna shredding her dress that first night. Razoring Jordan's T-shirt. Standing in the abandoned barn, holding the rusty metal claw. "I think she's really happy. She's met a guy." That wasn't a lie at least. *Though if Anna knew what her supposed best friend was doing, she wouldn't be happy for very long.*

"Oh, that's wonderful. She hasn't gone out with anyone since Mike, right?"

The pressure was growing more intense. Megan knew if she stayed on the phone much longer, she would blurt it all out, the whole tangled story. "Mom, I have to go," she said hurriedly. "Sweetie's . . . Sweetie's trying to eat the phone. I'll call you later, okay?"

She pressed end and let out a long breath. That was over at least.

Megan found Sweetie's little red halter hanging by the door and slipped it over his nose, buckling it behind his ears. She led him from the stall, and together, they paraded up and down the big barn floor. After three repetitions, Megan began to feel a little calmer. The walking was soothing, and Sweetie kept bumping her hand that was holding the lead rope. The little nose rubbing against her skin was almost like a massage.

The sun was a little higher now and was sending pale rays through the top of the hayloft. A thousand dust motes floated past, glittering like gold. At the other end of the barn, Megan heard the rumble of the big door sliding open.

Megan's breath caught at the sight of Jordan, and she couldn't help the huge, sloppy grin that spread over her face.

He didn't say anything as he approached. They stood a minute, just looking at each other.

"Morning," he said finally. He reached out and took her hand.

"Morning," Megan whispered. She suddenly felt shy. She could barely look at his face. It was too dazzling, like gazing at the sun. She wondered if he would kiss her again, then hated herself for thinking that. *Have you forgotten Anna entirely? You need to end this. End it right now.* "I got your note."

He nodded. Sweetie pushed his head in between the two of them and tossed it up and down a few times.

"I came looking for you," Jordan said. He stroked Sweetie's forelock. "I looked in the window of your cabin, but when I saw your bed was empty, I figured you'd be here."

Megan nodded. "I couldn't sleep."

"Me neither." He put his arms around her. "I was thinking about you."

His embrace was strong and comforting. Megan closed her eyes. "I was thinking about you too." *So much for ending it.*

This time, their lips met softly, like a butterfly's touch. Jordan kissed her several times, each time pausing for an instant, then pressing his mouth on hers again. Megan kissed him back, focusing only on his lips. It felt right, it felt good, better than anything she'd ever experienced. She wanted to stay in the barn, with him, forever.

But then she pushed herself away. "No," she managed. "We have to stop. We have to talk about this. About Anna."

Jordan didn't look surprised. "Okay."

They both took a deep breath. Beside them, Sweetie stamped his little foot.

"He wants to go out," Megan said. "Come with me?"

Jordan nodded. He slipped halters over Darryl's and Rosie's heads and led them both from their stalls. Megan followed him down the aisle, flipping Cisco's stall door open as she passed. Thomas had told her that he would follow the horses.

Out in the pasture, the horses trotted eagerly through the open gate, Darryl even cantering a little. Sweetie followed Rosie. Only two days old and already he could run alongside his mother. Megan watched them, her arms folded on the fence. Then she laid her head on her arms and said, "This can't work."

Jordan drew in his breath beside her. "Don't worry about Anna. I was never with her—I told you that."

"But she really, really likes you. She thinks you're in love with her." Megan's stomach twisted. She thought of the joy in Anna's eyes when Anna had first told her of Jordan.

Jordan made a gesture of impatience. "So, we flirted at the beginning. I'm allowed to change my mind. I don't know why we can't be together just because Anna wouldn't like it."

Megan shook her head and then took one of his hands. She looped her fingers through his, then turned his hand over. His skin was rough and dry. "There's something else I haven't told you," she said slowly.

Then haltingly, squinting out across the steadily brightening pasture, she told him the story of Mike, about him and Anna, the night of the party, and everything that had happened afterward.

"So this is the second time. It's like I made the worst mistake of my life . . . and now I'm doing it all over again." She couldn't look at him. She felt ashamed, weak. Like someone who just leapt on any guy her best friend liked.

Jordan gently put his arm around her shoulders. "It's not the same at all, Meg." His voice was low and intense. "That was just a fling—a one-time, dumb thing that happened. This is completely different. I really like you, Megan. I . . ."

She heard the click of his throat as he swallowed.

"I . . . I think I'm falling in love with you."

She drew in her breath and searched the blue depths of his eyes. His body was tense, as if bracing for a blow.

"Oh," Megan said. It was as if a tornado had churned up her insides and left all her feelings lying in different places. "I . . ."

"Don't say anything right now. All I'm trying to tell you is that sometimes you just can't control how you feel. I want to be with *you*, and I don't want to sneak around." He pulled her close so she was facing him.

"I want the same thing," Megan told him. She ran her hands up his arms and then laced her fingers behind his neck. "Jordan, look, this is all really confusing to me. But I want to be with you too." The words rang true in her ears. They felt good to say. It felt good to stand there, holding on to him. "I have to talk to Anna." She quailed at the thought. But she forced herself to say again, "I have to talk to Anna. I have to tell her everything."

She closed her eyes. Maybe Anna would understand that this was different from what happened with Mike. Maybe this wouldn't be the end of their friendship. Maybe. Megan clung to that thought. She had to believe this wouldn't be the end or she'd never do it.

She looked up at Jordan. She had the feeling he knew just what she was thinking. "Now. I have to do it now."

"Okay." He checked the latch on the gate, and they walked back toward the barn. "We're all supposed to pick cherries this morning. They moved a table over to the orchard, and we're going to have breakfast under the trees first."

Megan smiled. "That sounds fun."

"I guess they do it every year. Farm tradition and all."

"And everyone will be there?" She tugged the big barn door closed.

Jordan nodded.

Megan took a deep breath. "Okay, I'll talk to her then."

CHAPTER 10

The orchard was perched at the far end of the property—five acres of sour cherries, sweet cherries, apples, peaches, plums, and pears. The trees grew in neat rows, casting dappled shade on the soft grass beneath them. Someone had brought over the long picnic table from the front yard, and its blue-striped tablecloth fluttered a little in the wind.

Isaac and Robert were already sitting down, eating muffins. Robert had a red bandanna tied around his forehead, like Rocky Balboa gone wrong. Linda sat at the end. Megan was surprised to see her there—she didn't think the wheelchair could make it through the bumpy grass. Then she saw that Linda was sitting on an ordinary kitchen chair, with a walker beside her. Thomas must have helped her get down here.

"Come and get a muffin, you guys!" Sarah stood in the back of the newly repaired pickup, handing coolers of food down to Thomas on the ground. Today she had twirled her braids up into a crown on top of her head.

Megan winced at Sarah's cheerful greeting. She'd been hoping to slip in unnoticed, but now everyone looked up as she and Jordan approached the table side by side. Megan wondered what was written on her face.

She didn't look at Anna. Instead, she sat down and arranged her napkin in her lap, hoping to give herself a minute to recover. In some ways, it really didn't matter if Anna suspected something about her and Jordan. She was going to tell her everything anyway.

Robert passed the basket of muffins, and Megan took one. She just didn't want Anna to think she'd been sneaking around. She didn't want Anna to think this was like before. Megan cringed at the thought of hurting Anna, but then she steeled herself. She had to do it. She just had to

"Hey, where were you this morning?" Anna asked brightly, busily peeling an orange. Megan glanced at her. She looked cheerful and well rested, her skin glowing.

"I needed some air," Megan mumbled. She could hardly look at her friend.

"Here, this is a great orange." Anna handed her half. "Share it with me."

Thomas had seated himself at one end of the table. "The vet's coming to look at Samson this afternoon. Anyone want to volunteer to help out me and Dave?" He grinned at the silence that ensued. "Come on now, don't everyone talk at once."

"I'll do it," Isaac mumbled to his plate. "Volunteer my life." He cracked a small smile.

"Excellent! Robert, can you and Jordan take over Isaac's afternoon chores?"

"No problem." Robert's bandanna was askew.

Linda poured herself a second cup of coffee. "And don't forget the midsummer party tomorrow night. It's our big annual event. Most of the other local farmers and their summer help will be here." She paused, her eyes crinkling at the edges. "Perhaps even your good friend Mr. Coothy, Megan."

Megan laughed politely. The uncomfortable corn delivery seemed like it had been weeks ago, compared with all that had happened since. She made herself take a bite of her muffin.

"You're being so quiet," Anna said to Megan. She started on another orange. "Are you okay?"

"Um"—Megan shifted on her bench—"I . . . didn't get a lot of sleep last night. I was hot."

"Oh, I know. I was, like, dying in there." Anna's voice was happy. "Uncle Thomas, do you think we can get a fan for the cabin?" she called down to the other end of the table.

"I don't know, how many hours have you worked? Fans will only be distributed after you've logged another thousand hours."

Everyone laughed.

The strain of keeping a pleasant smile on her face was giving Megan a headache. She couldn't bear to look at Anna's happy face one minute longer.

I can't do it, she kept thinking. *I can't ruin her life all over again.* But then she would look at Jordan and think of how much she loved talking to him, sitting beside him, and touching his hand,

and she knew she had to confess everything. She wasn't going to hide like she had with Mike. This was different—this was real.

Dave rose and started clearing dishes, while Sarah hopped back into the pickup to receive the baskets of now-empty platters and coffee-stained cups. Meanwhile, Thomas helped Linda into the front seat of the truck, then organized everyone into a line. He handed out canvas-lined woven baskets, attached to long leather straps that slung across the wearer's chest and shoulder like a messenger bag.

"All right, everyone, listen up," Thomas instructed. "All the cherries are ripe, so you can pick from any tree. Dave and I have already placed two ladders per tree. Don't pick any overripe or rotten berries, obviously, and don't eat too many. And don't snack on the sour cherries. They'll knock you right off your ladders."

He pointed to big wooden crates lined up on the ground. "Empty your baskets into here. When they're full, Dave and I will take them back to the house in the truck and bring back new ones. If we all work together, we should be able to finish this by lunchtime."

There was a general milling around as everyone put on their baskets. Robert put the strap of his across his forehead and pranced around. Anna rolled her eyes and sighed in an irritated sort of way. She picked up her basket and slung it across her shoulder and chest. "He is so immature."

Megan nodded, barely hearing her. "Anna, I have to—" But her voice was too quiet.

"I'm going to snare that last tree," Anna said, already turning away. "Jordan!" She raised her voice and waved. "Come pick with me!" Megan noticed that she'd applied fresh lipstick, which gleamed greasily in the morning sun. The bright red looked out of place in the orchard. Megan closed her eyes.

When she opened them, Anna was already hurrying down the long row of trees. Megan slowly picked up a basket and put it on, then climbed the ladder of the nearest tree.

With her head and shoulders up in the branches, it was like being in some private tree world. The dark cherries hung like gifts. She spread her feet a little wider on the ladder rung to steady herself, and reached for a nearby cluster. She could hear Isaac talking to Dave in the next tree over, their voices overlaid with the rustling of the leaves. She picked for a few minutes, then Jordan appeared on the ladder beside her.

"What are you doing?" Megan teetered a little and clutched at a nearby branch. "I thought you were picking with Anna."

"I told her I had to get a drink." He leaned closer. "She tried to kiss me just now up in the tree. I didn't say anything, but I'll talk to her if you want me to."

Megan shook her head. "No. No, I have to do it myself." She let go of the ladder for a second and wiped her sweaty hands on the back of her shorts. "I screwed up once before. But I'm going to be honest with her this time."

"Okay." Jordan nodded. "Okay, I'm behind you." He reached out and touched her cheek, then pressed a soft kiss to her lips. "Good luck," he whispered.

Megan squeezed his hand quickly, then started to climb

down. She stopped. Her heart fell out of her chest. There, at the bottom of the ladder, looking up, was Anna, her face paper white. She'd heard them talking. She'd seen the kiss.

"Anna," Megan gasped. She scrambled down as quickly as she could with the picking basket.

Anna turned and ran.

"Wait, Anna, please," Megan called. She tripped off the last rung of the ladder and stumbled to her knees. Then she pulled off her basket and was on her feet, blood trickling from the scrape, as she ran after Anna.

Megan's mind whirled. It couldn't be worse. She had to explain, she had to. "Anna, please, wait up," she gasped out. Her heart was pounding against her ribs. The tree trunks flashed past. Up ahead, in the far reaches of the orchard, she saw Anna fall to her knees in the grass and bury her face in her hands.

Megan collapsed beside her, panting. Anna sobbed. The sound wrenched Megan's heart.

"Anna, please, I'm so sorry. Please, please let me explain." Already, tears ran down her own cheeks. She'd never felt so ashamed. "Anna, please, you have to listen. I was going to tell you. I was going to talk to you later this morning. This all just happened last night. Please listen!"

Anna's face blazed, wet with tears. "You! You traitor! My best friend—again! Stealing, stealing—" She dissolved into tears.

Megan could hardly see straight. She grasped her friend's hands tightly, trying to make Anna understand. "I know—I know how this looks. I—I don't know what to say, except that it just *happened* and you have to believe me that there is no way on earth I would have ever intentionally hurt you again. Please believe me. I love you, you're my best friend." She squeezed Anna's hands and stared into her face pleadingly.

Anna's sobs stilled. The tears stopped coursing down her cheeks. She gazed off down the long double row of fruit trees. "Tell me," she said quietly.

Megan told her—the day of Coothy and the truck break-down and her talk with Jordan. Then the campfire and the note. This morning in the pasture with Sweetie. She didn't mention her connection with Jordan that very first meeting in the kitchen. She didn't mention anything Jordan had said about Anna herself.

Anna was quiet now. Encouraged, Megan said, "Anna, this is totally different from Mike." She choked a little on his name. "This is . . ." She swallowed. "I feel like I've known him forever—like he understands me. I think this is it—the real thing." She waited. Anna's face was pale but composed.

After a moment, her friend spoke. "Does he love you?" Each word was distinct, falling on the silence, like raindrops hitting sand.

Megan nodded. "Yes," she said simply.

Anna jumped, as if she'd been pricked with a pin.

Megan shifted uncomfortably. She realized just how close she and Anna had been sitting and moved back a few inches.

"So, all that time, he wasn't really into me? He was into you?" Anna sounded calm now, almost casual, as if she were a reporter gathering information.

Megan looked away. "I—I don't know. Maybe he was into you at the start, but then—" Too late, she realized her blunder.

"—but then he met you," Anna finished quietly.

Megan couldn't think of anything to say. She looked down at her lap and twisted a few green blades of grass together between her fingers. "Do you hate me?"

Anna seemed to be expecting the question. "No. Well, maybe a little." She laughed dryly. "Who am I to stand in the way of love?"

"Thank you," Megan whispered. She reached out tentatively. Anna stiffened but did not protest as Megan hugged her. "I'm sorry," Megan said again.

"But not sorry enough to break up with him, right?" Anna's voice was steady, and she gazed at Megan with clear eyes.

Megan swallowed. "Right."

Anna considered Megan again, then climbed to her feet.

Megan reached out. "We're still friends, aren't we?" She knew how pitiful she sounded.

"I'm a big girl, Megan." Anna smiled. Walking back a few steps, she laid her hand on Megan's shoulder. "I can handle anything."

CHAPTER 11

Megan reached into the straw-filled hollow and pulled out two speckled eggs. Carefully, she placed them in the empty egg carton. Outside, the rooster crowed loudly. Megan could hear him attacking the door, trying to get in.

Around her ankles, the hens strutted and pecked, clucking out their discontent at the intrusion. They wanted to be left alone in their world. Megan understood perfectly. She wished she had a little place to retreat to—maybe a room, with blankets instead of straw, and all her books and her music and a store of popcorn and butter cookies. A retreat somewhere far from painful conversations and tricky friendships and tense meals. She placed another egg, this one a smooth brown, into the carton.

Jordan had been up on a ladder when she and Anna had emerged from the trees. Anna had volunteered to go back to the farmhouse and clean up the breakfast dishes, even though Sarah almost surely would have washed them already, and had hurried off toward the farm.

Megan plucked the last of the eggs from the nests. She emptied the old feed from the hens' bowls, dumping it out the tiny window where the songbirds would eat it. She rinsed and refilled the water dishes and swept up the old sawdust from the floor. The work was soothing and mindless. She poured new feed from the big paper sack in the closet and watched as the hens hopped onto the edges of the bowls, pecking rapidly at the shiny kernels.

Megan took up the eggs and the broom, then tentatively opened the people door out of the henhouse. The rooster gave a cry of triumph and flapped forward to strike at her legs with his sharp, spurred feet.

"Get away!" Megan cried, poking at him with the broom. He attacked the handle like it was the enemy he'd been waiting for all his life.

"You want to go for a ride?" A voice spoke beside Megan's ear.

Megan jumped, fumbling and almost dropping the double carton of eggs.

Anna raised her eyebrows. "Sorry." She stood very close to Megan. Megan wondered how she had crept up so quietly.

"It's okay." Megan hesitantly raised her eyes to Anna's face.

To her surprise, her friend was smiling. She'd changed her clothes and showered. Her wet hair was slicked back into a long braid that dangled halfway down her back. She wore a purple paisley tunic, and her toenails were freshly painted, ruby this time. Megan was suddenly aware of the dust on her face and her dirty, rumpled T-shirt.

"Want to go for a ride?" Anna asked again. She jingled a set of keys beside her face.

"Sure," Megan agreed enthusiastically. A wave of weepy thankfulness swept over her. *Anna isn't mad! She still wants to be friends!* Megan felt like crying with relief. She wanted to throw her arms around Anna and thank her for her incredibly mature and generous spirit, but she contented herself with a big, soppy grin. "Where are we going?"

"It's a surprise."

Anna thrust a plastic grocery sack into Megan's hands. Inside were Megan's swimsuit, a towel, and her sports sandals. Megan looked up quizzically, but Anna was already walking toward the farmhouse.

"Uncle Thomas said I could take the truck for a bit," she called back over her shoulder. "I thought you and me should get away and talk."

Megan hurried after her. It was almost twilight. "Um, where are we going?" she called hesitantly. "Maybe I'll run back to the cabin and wash up. And put these eggs in the kitchen."

Anna didn't pause or turn around. "No," she said. "Just leave them for a bit. They'll be fine."

In front of the farmhouse, Anna climbed into the truck and gunned the engine. Megan jumped in beside her, barely making it into the seat before Anna roared down the driveway. Megan's door was still open, and she leaned out to slam it.

Out of breath, she flopped safely back into the cab. Anna was driving with one hand and lighting a cigarette with the other. Megan blinked. "I didn't know you were smoking again."

Anna flicked a little silver lighter. "Guess you don't know everything, do you?" She put the lighter in the cup holder and puffed delicately.

Megan swallowed. "No, I don't," she said.

Anna didn't reply.

I shouldn't have come, Megan thought. She could see now that Anna was like a live time bomb sitting beside her.

"So, where are we going?" Megan asked again. She was surprised at how calm her voice sounded.

"Just somewhere we can talk." Anna sped down the road. She puffed at the cigarette rapidly. "You know, Meg, I was wrong this morning. I just got too worked up, you know?" She gestured with the cigarette, letting the smoke trail out the open window.

"Really?" Megan asked cautiously.

"Oh, yeah." Skillfully, Anna lit a new cigarette from the butt of the first. "I was surprised, definitely. But the more I think about it, the more I think that you and Jordan really would be cute together. Whoops!" She screeched the truck to a halt in the middle of the road, pitching Megan forward. If she hadn't been wearing her seat belt, she would have been thrown into the dashboard. Megan wasn't totally sure that wasn't the point.

"Almost missed the turn!" Anna turned the truck hard to the right and pulled onto a rough road but didn't slacken her speed.

Megan hung on to the handle above her door and braced

herself against the dashboard with her other hand. She began to feel scared. *Where are we going?*

Anna stopped in front of a copse of trees at the back of the field. It was full dark now. She dropped her cigarette to the floor of the truck and jumped out, disappearing into the woods.

Megan picked her way down. She could see the beam of Anna's flashlight bobbing against the trunks. She hurried to keep up. She didn't want to be left alone out in the lonely pasture.

Megan followed the purple print of Anna's back through the stand of trees and out to another overgrown field. The moon had risen, and Megan could see that the grass was knee high. Anna didn't look to see if Megan was following.

Megan struggled in her path, the long grass catching at her ankles.

"Hey, wait," she called out breathlessly. She broke into a stumbling run, trying to lift her feet high. Anna made a sharp turn and disappeared down into a little valley.

She's definitely acting strange, but she has had a big shock. You shouldn't be surprised. Hopefully, we can just work through it. Puffing and clutching the plastic bag in one hand, Megan followed and came to a big creek lined with brush. The water, murky under the night sky, rushed over rocks in foamy little waterfalls. In between, big, still pools reflected the moon. Anna was already standing on the bank, surveying the water, her hands on her hips.

Awkwardly, Megan crouched and edged sideways down the steep bank, grasping the branches of the shrubs for support, loose soil and small rocks sliding from under her sneakers. "Hey," she said as she finally made it to the bottom and stood next to Anna. "This creek is great. Did you used to come here when you were little?"

"All the time," Anna replied. Then suddenly, she whipped her tunic off over her head, revealing a white bikini. "Come on, let's swim!"

Megan started a little at the sudden change in her tone. "Um, in the dark?" She tried to sound casual instead of hesitant.

Anna raised her eyebrows. "Oh. Of course, I should've thought you'd be a pussy. . . ." Her voice trailed off.

"I'm not scared," Megan rejoined feebly. She set the grocery sack with her bathing suit down beside her. "It's just, um, are there snakes in there?" She thought of water moccasins undulating on the surface of the pool like smooth brown eels. Or the scene in *Lonesome Dove* where the Irish cowboy gets bitten by dozens of cottonmouths when he rides his horse into a river.

"Probably," Anna said cheerfully. Then she slipped gracefully into the water. Megan watched the flat surface, broken only by a few bubbles, for what seemed like a long time.

Finally, Anna came up, her head shiny as a wet seal's. She paddled over toward the bank and waded out, water streaming from her body. "Come on, come swim." Her eyes gleamed in the darkness. She tugged on Megan's hand. Her skin was clammy. Megan shuddered a little. The thought of going in that cold, black water was repellent.

"No, thanks." She shifted a little on the rock she was sitting on. "I'll just watch you."

"Oh, come on!" Anna urged. She backed up, still holding Megan's hand. Megan felt herself slide forward a little.

She held on to the side of the rock. "I said no!" Her voice was louder than she intended.

A film dropped over Anna's face. Megan bit her lip, but she forced herself to stay on the rock. Nothing could make her get into that inky water.

Then Anna shrugged. "Okay." She turned and slid sinuously under the water again.

Megan let out her breath, watching Anna swim across the pool, up to the water rushing over a collection of boulders. Like a creature born of this place, Anna delicately picked her way over the rocks, until she reached another large pool of water on the opposite side.

She's still mad. Pissed off. Not surprising, of course. Just stay calm. Let her get it out. Megan shivered slightly and rubbed her upper arms, which were pimpled with goose bumps. She wondered how long Anna wanted to stay out here. She must be freezing from swimming, and they weren't doing much talking, if that's what was really the purpose of their trip.

Idly, Megan ran her fingers over the edge of the rock she sat on. A chunk came off in her hand and she looked at it, surprised. It wasn't granite, as she'd thought, but some sort of hard, crumbly claylike stuff. It smelled like pottery class.

"Shale."

Megan started, dropping the rock, which fell into the water with a *plunk*.

Anna stood behind her.

"How'd you get up there?" Megan asked a little shakily.

"Walked." Anna perched beside Megan, and clasped her arms around her wet knees, looking like a wood sprite in the unearthly silver moonlight. "That's shale, that crumbly rock. It's supposed to be good for your skin too. Here, watch."

Anna reached down and broke off a piece as Megan had, then laid it on the rock beside her and pounded it swiftly with another, harder rock. The shale broke into powdery chunks, which Anna then ground and mixed with creek water until she had a smooth clay. She scooped it into her hands and methodically smeared it all over her face. *It looks like a Halloween mask*, Megan thought, as Anna's bright eyes peered out from the rough mud.

"Here, you try it." Anna reached toward Megan's face with a handful.

Megan was tempted to say no, but she let Anna smear the stuff on her. As her friend's hands moved gently over her skin, Megan felt herself relax in spite of herself. The mud was actually kind of soothing. So close to hers, Anna's face was suddenly familiar and dear, like that of a sister.

"Cool," Megan said, touching her own face gently. The mud was already hardening, making it hard to talk. "Where'd you learn about that?" She had to articulate carefully to get the words out. "I had no idea you were such an earth mother."

To Megan's relief, Anna laughed. "There's a lot you don't know about me."

"Really? We've been best friends since first grade," Megan said, surprised, and stretched out her legs.

"Well, there's stuff I can tell you, if you want to know." Anna's voice dropped conspiratorially, and she edged closer to Megan.

"Ooh, what?" Megan giggled, a little zing of anticipation running through her. She half expected Anna to offer her something delicious and forbidden, like a pilfered brownie or her mother's lipstick, the way she had when they were little.

Anna's lips curled in a secret smile. "Well, stuff about your new boyfriend, for one thing." Her breath smelled like stale cigarette smoke.

Megan took a minute to register that Anna was talking about Jordan.

"Like what?" she asked.

Anna licked her lips until they glistened. "Well, he is just *huge*," she whispered, even though there was no one around for miles. "Seriously hung. And he loves you to—"

Megan grimaced and held her hands out in front of her. "Stop, okay?" She pushed herself back a few feet on the rock. "I don't want to know that stuff."

But Anna crawled toward her on her hands and knees. She pushed her face into Megan's. "Don't be such a prude. Jordan won't like that. He's an *animal*, Meg, an absolute *beast*." A faint spray of spit flew from her lips. "He was always trying to put his hand—"

"Anna, quit it!" Megan got to her feet. "I said I don't want to hear stuff like that." She felt faintly dirty.

Anna sat back on her heels, looking wounded. "I just thought you'd want to know. Common courtesy and all." She got to her feet, brushing off her knees. "Fine with me if you don't." Her voice was stiff.

"Don't be mad," Megan pleaded. "I'm sorry. You've been amazing about all this." She took her friend's hand and squeezed it. Anna's flesh was icy cold. "Thanks for understanding," Megan said. She meant it.

Anna nodded and shivered. "You know," she said in a small voice. "It seems like people are always leaving me. First Dad. Then Mike. Now Jordan."

Megan crumbled another piece of shale in her fingers. Anna didn't bring up her father very often. Megan knew it was a hard topic.

"After Dad left, I was sure no one else would ever love me again," Anna went on. She rested her head on her updrawn knees and sighed. "Until I met Jordan. I really thought he was the one." Her voice broke slightly.

Megan looked at her more closely in the moonlight. Anna's lips were purple, and her shoulders were shaking.

"You're freezing," Megan said with concern. "Come on, let's go back."

Anna nodded. They splashed creek water on their faces to rinse off the mud, then Megan put her arm around her shoulders. All of Anna's energy seemed to have drained from her, and she allowed herself to be led back through the pasture.

Anna's legs were shaking by the time they made it to the truck.

Megan paused. "You'd better let me drive."

"Yeah," Anna almost-whispered. "I'm beat."

Megan draped her towel around Anna's shoulders before starting the engine. She cranked the heater up full blast, and Anna leaned her head against the seat, closing her eyes.

Megan managed to get them back to the farm with a minimum of stalls, drawing on every ounce of knowledge about driving a stick that she remembered from driver's ed. Anna was quiet during the drive, and her eyes were still closed when Megan parked in front of the dark farmhouse. She looked like a little child, enveloped in the big towel.

On an impulse, Megan reached out and stroked her friend's damp, tangled hair. "We're going to get through this, you know," she said softly.

Anna's eyelids flew open like window shades. Megan saw that the white of her right eye was blood red. She inhaled sharply.

"Shit, Anna, what's wrong with your eye?" she gasped.

Anna blinked, throwing off the towel. "I must have burst a blood vessel." She opened the truck door. "Happens when I'm stressed out." She climbed out. "Come on. I'm sleepy."

Megan trailed Anna to the cabin, still trying to shake the image of Anna's red eye peering at her. She reached for the lantern as soon as she got in.

"I'm not even going to brush my teeth, I'm so tired," she said to Anna as she switched on the light.

She turned to her bed and pulled back the top cover. Then she screamed, dropping the lantern, which went out as it crashed to the floor. She screamed again, stumbling backward until she fell on Anna's bed.

"What? What?" Anna was beside her now, flashlight in hand.

"On the bed!" Megan pointed, her other hand clamped over her mouth. She willed herself not to throw up.

Anna played the beam from the foot of the bed, past the gray blanket, up to the pillow. "Oh my God!" she shrieked. There on the pillow, a clutch of tiny cockroaches squirmed, writhing over each other in a dark, brown-green mass. "Jesus!"

"What do we do?" Megan moaned. "How did they get in?"

Anna played the beam of the flashlight up to the wall. "There—that's how."

Megan saw a thin crack in the wooden plank just above her bed. The dark night was just visible through the break. She moaned and buried her head in Anna's pillow. She couldn't stand one more second of those waving antennae and flat, slimy bodies. "Get rid of them, please, please."

"Ew, no." Anna backed away. "I'm not touching those things. That's too disgusting. And all over your pillow!"

Megan swallowed hard and got up from the bed. "Open the door," she said.

Anna pushed the screen door wide. Moving fast, before she could think about what she was doing, Megan scooped up the pillow—*don't dump them on the floor!*—and flung it out the front door. She couldn't see what happened to the roaches in the dim light, but the pillow landed with a soft *flump* on the dirt in front of the porch. Gradually, her pulse slowed.

Anna started busily shoving clothes and blankets into a duffel bag.

"What are you doing?" Megan asked.

"I'm not sleeping here anymore." Anna folded a blue towel into the bag. "Roaches only like things that are dirty—like your pillow. I mean, why would they be there and not on my bed?"

"Because of that crack in the wall, remember?"

Anna unhooked her toiletry bag from its place by the door. "But why would they just stay there? Did you think of that? I mean, would they just hang out on your pillow if they weren't attracted by some smell or something?"

"Are you saying I'm dirty?" Megan felt her hair. It was a little oily, but she'd just washed it that morning. She felt vaguely ashamed, as if she'd been caught picking her nose. *But I haven't* done *anything!*

Anna zipped the bag briskly. "Sorry. I don't want to hurt your feelings." She shrugged. "I'm sure Uncle Thomas will let me sleep at the house." She moved toward the door.

Megan panicked at the thought of being left alone out there in the cabin, all of those roaches right outside, maybe already crawling back up the walls or under the screen door, trying to get back in. . . .

"Wait, Anna!" She clutched her friend's sleeve. Anna looked down at Megan's hand pointedly. Megan took her hand away. "Please, please don't go. I don't know why the roaches were on my pillow, but I'll wash it, okay? And we can put some duct tape over the crack. Please! I don't want to stay out here by myself." She hated the cringing abjectness in her voice.

Anna regarded her steadily. Her bad eye looked like a pool of blood. She set down her bag and sighed. "Fine. But you'd better wash *all* your bedding—tonight. Whatever those bugs liked on your pillow is still there. And take a shower."

Megan felt a stupid urge to cry, whether with thankfulness that Anna was staying or misery, she didn't know. "Thanks. Here's the tape." She pulled a roll of duct tape, something her mother said you should never travel without, from her bag and set it on the bedside table. Then she pulled the blanket and sheet off the bed and dumped them both on the floor.

"Oh, and Megan?" Anna spoke from behind her.

Megan turned around.

"You'd better wash your hair, too."

The cabin was dark and Anna was asleep when Megan returned from the farmhouse two hours later, clean from the shower and bearing an armload of freshly washed laundry. She made up her bed, dragging from weariness, and climbed between the clean sheets. Layers of sleep were beginning to fold in over her when she remembered the crack. She pushed herself up, meaning to make sure Anna had taped it thoroughly. The crack was still open. And the roll of duct tape sat on the table where she'd left it. Anna had just gone to bed, as if she wasn't worried about the roaches at all.

CHAPTER 12

"Come on, little guy, come on." Megan kept her voice low and steady, but friendly, as she urged Sweetie into his stall. The morning sun was hot, and the little foal's fur was wet on his chest and behind his ears. He smelled like a damp wool sweater, an odor that Megan found oddly pleasant.

She and Sweetie had been working together for over an hour while Rosie grazed nearby, but Megan sensed the little horse was tiring. He was making a lot of progress, though. He had already learned not to chew on the halter or lead rope and not to turn his head around when he was being led. Now Megan was working on picking up his feet, which Sweetie was not very fond of. He had a lot of strength in those bony little legs and had very nearly stamped Megan's toes many times.

But Sweetie had also developed a slight fear of the drain that ran in front of his stall and was reluctant to step over it.

Maybe he's afraid of the metal grille covering it, Megan thought.

Sweetie balked again as she tried to lead him into the stall, even though Rosie was already waiting calmly within. He was hungry, Megan knew, and wanted his mother. This only increased his anxiety, and he pulled back on the lead rope, his little head twisting up and away, his eyes wide.

"Now, now," Megan soothed. "Easy." She knew instinctively that he shouldn't be forced but that he would only get over his fear by walking over the drain. The last thing she wanted was for him to develop a bad association with his stall.

Megan thought for a moment, then tied Sweetie to a rack across the aisle. She went down to the feed room and returned with a cup of sweet feed, the honey-coated grain that the foal loved.

She sprinkled a handful of the grain on the floor just beyond the drain, and then another handful a few feet farther away. Then she led Sweetie over to it.

"See?"

She showed him the feed, and he eyed the drain for a long moment, then very tentatively stretched out his neck. He delicately ate the kernels, then noticed the second handful. He would have to step over the drain to get to it.

Megan watched him thinking about it. Sweetie raised one hoof, then set it down, looked at the grain, then, as she held the rope loosely, stepped over the drain. Megan patted his neck as he ate the treat, but inside, she was jumping up and down.

As she closed the door and hung the rope up, she thought to herself that nothing in the world was as satisfying as those little moments of triumph. Sweetie had gotten over the drain and he hadn't been scared. She was so proud of him.

Humming happily to herself, Megan headed down the barn aisle. Lunch would be ready in a few minutes, and she was on serving duty, since Anna and Sarah were cooking. There had been no discussion of the cockroach incident when they woke this morning—just the usual chat about the day. The blood had retreated from Anna's eye.

Outside on the dusty path, Megan saw Jordan heading toward her, and her heart gave a little leap. He looked like a golden god. "Hi," she said. "How'd you know I was here?"

He smiled at her and touched her hair. "Where else would you be?" He took her hand, intertwining his fingers with hers as they walked toward the farmhouse. "I like this," he said.

"Lunch?"

He laughed. "No, being able to hold your hand. I'm really glad everything's out in the open."

Megan nodded. "Me too."

Jordan must have sensed something in her voice, because he glanced down at her. "Yeah, how'd it go with Anna?"

Megan shrugged. The white of the farmhouse showed now through the trees ahead. "Okay, I guess. She says everything's cool, and she's speaking to me at least." An image of Anna's bloody eye flashed through her mind. "She might need a few days to adjust."

Jordan nodded. "That's understandable."

The table was under the trees and set for lunch, with a plate of carrot sticks and pepper slices in the middle. No one was outside, though she heard Anna's and Sarah's voices floating out from the kitchen. Gently, she tried to extract her hand from Jordan's, and he looked down at her quizzically.

Megan smiled apologetically. "Sorry," she whispered, pulling away.

Jordan glanced at the farmhouse, then quickly drew her in toward him, pressing a kiss to her lips. "All right for now," he said. "But that party is tonight, and we're dancing. I don't care who's there." His blue eyes were intense.

"We'll dance," Megan promised, holding both of his hands.

The screen door banged, and they both looked over. Anna came down the steps with a platter of sandwiches, followed by Sarah with a bowl of strawberries. Megan dropped Jordan's hands as if they were on fire.

"Hey, I was supposed to serve," she said, hurrying toward them with her cheeks flaming.

"No worries. We were ready a little early," Sarah said, shifting the plates around on the table to make room for the sandwiches. Megan envied her suddenly, so confident, secure in her relationship, happy in her job.

Anna silently piled carrot sticks onto her plate. Without waiting for the others, she sat down and started to eat. Megan looked at Sarah. "Where's everyone?"

Sarah stared into the distance, thinking. "Let's see—Dave's stocking horse feed, Thomas is harrowing oats, and Linda's taking a nap in the house. She wants to be fresh for the party tonight. And Robert and Isaac are picking up party supplies in town. We're eating in shifts today, especially since I've got the party food to cook." She held out the plate of sandwiches. "You guys want tuna or ham and cheese?"

Megan took a tuna sandwich and went to sit beside Anna. Her friend was eating stolidly, as if she were completing an assignment.

"I had the best morning with Sweetie," Megan said, biting a corner off her sandwich. She watched Jordan tactfully sit down at the other end of the table, beside Sarah.

Anna said nothing at first. She'd already finished a ham and cheese sandwich, Megan noticed, and was starting on a second one. "What happened?" Anna asked after a long moment.

Megan could tell it was an effort for her to get the words out. Regret and love almost choked Megan, and it took her a second to answer. "I got Sweetie to step over this drain he was afraid of." She made her voice cheerful. She felt like Anna had been wounded and it was up to her to make her friend better.

Sarah stood in alarm. "What is it?"

Dave was running down the path toward them, a feed scoop in his hand. Megan was surprised—no one ran around here.

"The foal's out," he said between pants, his big face bright red. "Stall was unlatched. I got the mare in, but the foal must be down by the road now."

The road! Megan's heart thudded. She flashed on the story

about Aunt Linda's old dog—the one that got hit on the road.

"What do we do?" she cried.

"Thomas is down there, but the foal won't come to him," Dave said. "Megan, we need your help. Maybe he'll come to you. Here, I brought you some sweet feed—get going! Jordan and I'll go down and try to stop traffic."

Dave's words were like an electric jolt. Megan started running. She'd only gone a few yards down the gravel driveway before she heard someone running after her. Then Anna's cool voice spoke. "Here, you forgot the feed." Anna thrust the scoop into Megan's hand. "Don't worry. You'll get him."

Anna's voice flowed like a tonic over Megan's vibrating nerves. Megan nodded. "You're right. He'll be okay," she heard herself say. In the far reaches of her mind, she wondered briefly why Anna was being so nice. Megan knew she was still mad. Maybe she was getting over it.

Together, they ran out to the road. Thomas was in the center of the blacktop, holding a coffee can of grain toward the foal, who stood coyly about thirty feet away.

"Here, here," Thomas crooned soothingly, rattling the grain can.

But Sweetie took no notice. Instead, he stepped delicately to one side and nosed the dotted yellow center line.

Megan heard the car before she saw it—a loud muffler buzzing in the quiet like an oncoming bee swarm. Then she saw the sun glinting off the windshield. It was going too fast—she could see that already.

"Stop!" Thomas yelled, waving his arms from the shoulder, but it was too late. The car zoomed up the road and Megan prayed, willing Sweetie not to step forward into its path.

The next thing she knew, the car was past them and the little horse still stood at the side of the road, his big eyes looking at them wonderingly.

"He's okay, Meg," Anna said. Megan nodded mutely. Thomas slipped Sweetie's little red halter into her hand.

"Sweetie," Megan called calmly. "Hi, boy." The foal looked at her. "What are you doing out here, silly boy?" Megan asked him conversationally. She sensed it was best not to let him know anything was wrong. She needed to convince him that she was the most interesting thing here, not the road or the miles of freedom unfurling before him.

Casually, she rattled the feed scoop. She walked, slowly but confidently, toward Sweetie, keeping up an easy patter while holding out the feed.

"You want a treat, baby?" she asked.

He took a step toward her, sniffing the air.

She was only about five feet away now, and she knew he could smell the grain. She stopped.

"Well, come on over here and get it." She waited. Her body language said she had all the time in the world.

The foal took one step, then another. The allure of the grain was irresistible. He took one last step and thrust his nose into the scoop.

Working calmly and swiftly, Megan buckled the halter over

his head, then breathed a huge sigh of relief. She buried her face in his furry neck as he munched the grain.

"Very well done, Megan. You handled that like a natural horsewoman," Thomas said, taking the lead rope.

Megan realized her knees were trembling. They all walked back toward the farmhouse, but she didn't fully relax until they were safely on the driveway.

Megan didn't think she could eat any more lunch. Thomas led Sweetie toward the barn, while Megan and Anna walked over to the chicken coop. They were supposed to collect eggs this afternoon, and it was late.

Silently, Anna opened the coop door and let Megan pass through. Most of the hens and the rooster were outside, pecking around in the grass for insects. Just one fat red chicken sat in a box in the corner, feathers fluffed out, clucking quietly.

Megan had plucked two warm, spotted eggs from a low nest box before Anna spoke. "You left the door unlatched, didn't you?"

Megan winced. She placed the eggs in her collecting carton before answering, "I don't think so, but I don't know how else they could've gotten out." She pictured herself celebrating Sweetie's triumph over the drain, then closing the door behind him and hanging up his halter. But had she slid the latch? It was possible she'd forgotten in all her excitement. Megan took a large brown egg from another nest.

"So, basically, it's your fault."

Megan dropped the egg. Viscous yellow splattered the wall.

"Shit," she whispered. She knelt to gather up the fragmented shell.

"Good thing you caught him," Anna went on. Megan glanced over. Her friend was rolling an egg around between her palms. "If he'd gotten hit, it would've been your fault too, you know."

"I know." Megan felt sick. She watched Anna toss the egg in the air. The shell had an odd greenish tinge.

"Your fault. He could've died." Anna tossed the egg again. And this time let it drop.

CHAPTER 13

"Oh, come on, don't you want to wear it?" Anna shook the lacy white shirt in front of Megan as she sat on her bed later that evening. Anna wore only her bra and jeans, and for the billionth time, Megan wondered how she got her stomach to look like that.

"I don't feel like dressing up." Megan plucked at the scratchy blanket.

Despite the prospect of a party, a depression had settled over her after egg collecting. She knew it was because of the Sweetie incident. Anna was right—it *was* her fault. She'd gotten overconfident and, *boom*, screwed up. She was a loser. Megan heaved a gusty sigh and lay back on the mattress.

"Stop being such a downer!" Anna pitched the shirt at Megan. "You'll look gorgeous in that. I'm going to wear this one." She held up a clingy black top. "And a black bra—it'll be perfect."

Megan watched as her friend wafted around the little cabin.

Anna was in a marvelous mood. She brushed her long black hair and put on a pair of long silver earrings that brushed her neck.

"What do you think?"

Anna twirled.

Megan had to smile. "Really nice."

"I think he'll like it." Anna turned back to the tiny, spotted mirror and leaned in to apply a deep berry lipstick.

Megan's heart skipped a beat. "Um . . . who?"

Anna capped the lipstick. "Robert, of course." She blotted her mouth on a tissue.

Megan sat up. "I thought you didn't like him."

"What gave you that idea?" Anna shot her a quizzical look, then breezed over to her trunk. She extracted a hot pink silk flower on a bobby pin and slid it into her hair just over one ear.

Megan opened her mouth, then closed it again. Anna turned around, holding another flower in her hand, this one bright yellow.

"Look, this is perfect for you." She leaned over and clipped it into Megan's hair. Megan caught a whiff of her lemon perfume.

Anna dragged Megan over to the mirror. Together, they gazed at their flower-bedecked reflections. Anna was right. The big yellow flower contrasted perfectly with her chestnut hair.

Megan grinned at her friend, her heart suddenly lifting. "You're right. Thank you."

Anna nudged her. "You're welcome. Now would you please put on that shirt so we can go already?"

Megan laughed and nodded. "Okay, just give me a minute."

The Sweetie thing was over with. There was no sense in sitting around dwelling on it. Anna was right. She might as well go to the party and have a good time.

Jordan was coming up the path just as they were leaving. Megan automatically tensed—her autoresponse these days—and glanced at Anna, but her friend's flow of chatter didn't break.

"Hey," Jordan said as he approached. "Came to see if you guys were ready."

"We are! And I lent Megan my shirt. How do you like it?" Anna burbled.

Jordan smiled shyly at Megan. "Nice," he said. His eyes ran over her figure, and Megan felt her cheeks grow pink. She realized it was the first time a guy had looked at her like that with Anna standing there beside her. They were usually looking at Anna.

They all walked to the house together, Megan in the middle. Anna pointed out a cluster of yellow buttercups and a tiny green frog. They passed the garden and admired the corn, which looked like it had grown a foot practically overnight.

Megan felt enchantment in the air, as if this evening was guaranteed to be filled with perfect happiness. Anna content, Jordan holding her hand. It was a beautiful night, and they were going to a party. She looked up at Jordan and squeezed his hand. He put his arm around her shoulders and pulled her in close as they walked.

"Ooh, look!" Anna pointed ahead.

The farmhouse was transformed by strings and strings of

white lights: on the bushes, over the porch railings, on the trees. Torches stood all around the perimeter of the lawn, flaring in the twilight, and the long table from the kitchen had been moved out to the grass next to the picnic table. They were both covered with white cloths, and even from a distance, Megan could see they were loaded with good things to eat: caramel corn, olives, pickles, cherry tomatoes, little sandwiches, homemade hot pretzels, sliced peaches and strawberries, jugs of iced tea and cold cider.

Groups of people were already scattered on the lawn, talking, holding glasses. Robert and Dave tacked up a loose strand of lights, while Thomas stood talking with Isaac and a craggy figure Megan recognized as Mr. Coothy. She swallowed and hoped he wouldn't spot her with all the other people around. Nearby, Dee, Murray, and Charles from the farmers' market were filling plates at the food table.

On the porch, a band with a mandolin, banjo, and guitar was warming up. Linda rolled across the grass toward them.

"The last to arrive!" she called. She was wearing a soft, airy lavender dress, and her white hair shone platinum in the flaring light.

"It took us a while to get dressed," Anna explained in a genuinely friendly voice.

Megan smiled to herself. This evening *was* enchanted.

"You girls look lovely," someone said from behind them. They turned around to see a surprisingly handsome Thomas in a white shirt with the sleeves pushed up, holding a tray of hamburger patties. Beside him, Sarah balanced a big stack of buns. Megan thought she looked like a ballerina in her simple black sundress, with her long hair pulled back in a loose bun.

Anna hugged her uncle. "Thanks, Uncle Thomas." Then she pulled away and hurried off past the group without a backward glance.

"We'll be grilling in a few minutes!" Thomas called after her. "If Sarah doesn't drop the patties in the coals like last time." He gave Sarah a mischievous look, and she rolled her eyes at Megan and Jordan.

"If you smell burning, it's all him," she said to them as Thomas went over to the big charcoal grill.

Megan and Jordan were left standing alone. He twined his arm around her waist, and they slowly strolled toward the food table. "That caramel corn looks good," Megan said.

"I saw Sarah making it earlier." Jordan picked a few crunchy, golden pieces from the basket. "She made her own caramel."

Megan nibbled on a handful. "You can do that?"

"Yeah. She said all you do is burn sugar and melt it together with butter—" Jordan stopped talking and looked at something over Megan's shoulder. Megan turned.

Anna stood pressed up against Robert, laughing loudly at something he'd said.

"Stop! You are so kidding," Megan heard her say. Her voice carried easily over the crowds. Robert looked surprised but pleased. He grinned tentatively.

"No, really. Two twenty-five," he said.

"Stop! Stop!" Anna sounded as if he'd just told her he was going into space. "Isaac!" She grabbed Isaac, who was standing beside her. "Robert can bench two twenty-five. Isn't that *incredible*?"

"I thought she didn't like him," Jordan said.

Megan shrugged. "People change." They looked at each other, knowing something was askew but not quite sure what. The band finished tuning up and swung into a bluegrass tune.

"You want to dance?" Jordan asked.

"I don't know how to dance to this kind of music." Megan hung back. "It's old-timey."

"Whatever." Jordan grabbed her hand. "We'll look stupid together."

Megan laughed and let him pull her over to where Dave and Sarah and a few other couples were already dancing. Megan knew there was no way she could replicate their steps, which looked like some kind of jig, but Jordan swung her around, and they did a few twirls. Jordan's face drew near hers and then farther away as he spun her to the twangy beat. Megan realized it didn't matter what she looked like—she was having fun.

They danced for a while, then drifted over for burgers, then danced again. Gradually more and more couples surrounded them and the music grew louder. Megan saw Thomas dancing with Dee, Murray dancing with Sarah, and Isaac dancing with a tall brown-haired girl. On the far steps of the porch, Dave sat next to Mr. Coothy—both of them wearing identical don't-make-me dance expressions.

Megan thought of nothing but Jordan and the music. She only saw his smiling face and felt his hands on her arms, shoulders, and waist. He kissed her as they swung closer together, and she laughed with delight.

Gradually, Megan became aware of a disturbance. It was Anna, her hair tumbling down her back and her shirt askew, laughing loudly and trying to grind with Robert, who was holding her to keep her from falling to the ground. Anna's face was flushed. Her shirt had pulled up in the back and hung too far down her front, exposing her lacy black bra. "Come on," she was saying. "Come on." She stretched up, trying to kiss Robert, rubbing her hands across his shoulders and down his arms. He kissed her back, but Megan could tell he was self-conscious with everyone watching.

Megan reached Anna the same time Thomas did. Linda followed behind. Thomas leaned in close, and Megan knew he was trying to smell Anna's breath for alcohol.

"Anna, honey, you need to cool it," he said gently.

Anna grinned sloppily. "Uncle Thomas! *You* need to cool it." She wasn't slurring her words, but Megan had seen how drunk she could get at parties. She looked like she was on her way to passing out.

Linda wheeled herself closer. "Anna, you're drunk," she said sharply.

Megan drew in her breath. *Linda, stay out of this. She could get ugly.*

"Shut up, you crippled—"

Megan pushed her way over and grabbed Anna's hand, wincing at the hurt on Linda's face.

"It's all right, Linda. I'll just—" What Megan was going to do she didn't know, but she needed to get Anna away from this situation before things got even worse. "I'll just help Anna fix her hair," she finished lamely, and led her friend inside the house to the bathroom.

"What is going on with you?" Megan hissed as soon as they were alone. She tried to detangle Anna's long locks with her fingers. "How did you get booze in here?" But even as she spoke, she realized that she still didn't smell alcohol on her friend. And Anna's eyes weren't glazed or glassy. On the contrary, they were sharply alert.

Anna straightened her shirt. "Why are you getting in the way of my fun? I'm just having a good time, and now you're over here mommying me."

"I just . . . well, you said that thing to Linda. And Thomas was getting mad." *And everyone here is looking at you.*

"So?" Anna challenged her. "How do you know he's not mad at you, too?"

Megan blinked, taken aback. "I'm not the one making out all over the place."

"Oh, yes, you are." Anna leaned in. "You guys are practically licking each other up and down out there. It's disgusting."

Megan opened her mouth and closed it, stunned by the sheer unfairness of her accusation.

Anna's voice changed, and she smiled widely, showing her teeth. "I know you want me to have a good time too. Just like you, right? And I'm going to. I'm going to have a great time, Megan."

Anna pulled a cigarette out of her jeans pocket and lit it with her little silver lighter. She inhaled, then blew the smoke into Megan's face, leaned over, and planted a big kiss on her cheek. Then she walked away.

A twinge of the same fear she'd felt last night by the creek rose up in Megan's throat. She pushed it back and found her way over to Jordan, who was leaning against the porch railing, his hands in his pockets.

"Everything okay?" he asked. He held out a little daisy. "I found this for you."

Megan didn't want to admit what had just happened with Anna. Her insides felt cold thinking about it. Megan longed for a hot bath and her bed at home. Instead, she took Jordan's hand.

"Let's go, okay? It's starting to rain." A few drops were falling. The moon was hidden by clouds.

"Yeah, let's get some cake. Sarah's cutting it now."

"No, seriously, can we leave? I don't feel very well." She thought of Anna's calm, grating voice.

Jordan stooped, his eyes dark with concern. "You look pale, Meg."

"I do?" she responded mindlessly. Lots of people were still dancing, but a few others were gathering their things too.

"Thanks, Linda," Jordan called as they walked past her. "Night."

"Night, you guys." She waved.

Near the edge of the lawn, Anna was leaning up against Robert, saying something in his ear. He had a big goofy grin on his face. When Anna saw Megan and Jordan coming, she waved.

"Don't wait up for me, Meg!" she called. She broke into giggles, and she and Robert disappeared into the darkness.

Megan and Jordan walked on in the light rain. Megan fought down a rising sense of anger that Anna's weird mood had kept her from enjoying a perfect evening with Jordan. *But you're here now. Just try to forget it,* she told herself.

Jordan walked her back to the cabin. At the steps, he started to say something but stopped. Gently, he put his hand on the back of her neck. Megan closed her eyes as his lips met hers, slow, smooth, hot, as if he had all the time in the world and the kiss was never going to end. She never wanted it to.

At last they broke apart. Jordan glanced at the cabin. "Should I . . . come inside?"

Yes! her mind yelled, but a wiser, more responsible Megan spoke instead. "I don't know . . . maybe not yet?"

Jordan smiled, and she knew he understood. He leaned forward and kissed her again, then turned back toward the farmhouse. She reluctantly let his hand slip from her fingers. He receded down the path. But before he was out of sight, just a shadowy figure now, he blew her a kiss.

Megan floated inside the cabin, by herself, since Anna was who knew where with Robert. She pulled on her big T-shirt and sweat shorts and, skipping a washup, got into bed, pleasantly tired. The bed felt almost homey and the sound of the gentle rain on the tin roof comforting, as if this had been her room all her life. She slept.

∾

Much later, in the thin light of dawn, Megan awakened to the sound of running footsteps outside her window. Anna lay in her bed, deeply asleep.

There were more footsteps, then someone pounded at the door. Megan sat up, pushed the covers aside, and opened the screen.

Thomas stood on the porch, boots over his striped pajamas, holding a coil of rope. Dave stood at the bottom of the steps, wearing sweatpants and carrying more rope.

"Get some shoes on, Megan," Thomas said, his voice tense. "The foal's out again—we found the door open. He's not on the farm property—we're going to check the old pastures. We need you in case he won't come to us."

Across the room, Anna groaned in her sleep and rolled over. Megan shoved her feet into her sneakers. Her sleepy fingers fumbled the laces.

Outside, it was cool and everything was wet with dew. Megan's head felt unusually foggy. She shook it, trying to wake up. She followed Thomas and Dave around the cabin and through the open meadow. "Sarah and Isaac are checking the woods," Dave shouted over his shoulder.

Wet grasses whipped at her shins as they passed the sheep pastures. Megan was so sleepy, but still she ran. Dave and Thomas pulled ahead.

Why can't I wake up?

As they approached the abandoned barn, Thomas and Dave came to a stop beside Sarah and Isaac. They were all looking down the long hill that sloped away from the buildings.

Megan stumbled up to them and followed their gaze. In an instant, all the sleepiness was shocked out of her system.

A motionless brown form lay at the bottom of a long skid track, wet with mud and damp leaves.

Sweetie.

Megan lurched forward, running down the hill, tripping, almost falling herself. At the bottom, she collapsed onto her knees and laid a hand on Sweetie's soft brown shoulder. His eyes glared sightlessly up at the gray morning sky, his legs twisted beneath him. Megan bent her head to the ground and wept.

CHAPTER 14

Megan felt a hand on her back. She looked up into Thomas's sympathetic eyes.

"Megan. He must have tripped and fallen."

"But . . . how? . . ." Megan allowed herself to be led back up the hill. The others were sober-faced, looking down at the body, then away, as if they couldn't bear to see the twisted form lying in the mud either.

Isaac stuffed his hands into his pockets, cleared his throat.

"He got out, I guess," Dave was saying when Anna panted up, wearing a sweatshirt over her pajamas, her hair still mussed from sleep.

"Hey, what's up? I rushed out . . . ," she said, out of breath. "What's—" She caught sight of the body. "Oh, no." She looked closer. "Oh, shit, is that *Sweetie*? Is he okay? What happened?"

Megan turned on her. She couldn't bear the avid curiosity in her friend's voice. "He's dead, Anna! He fell. . . ." Her voice cracked.

"Oops," Anna said.

"Come on. We're not helping anything standing here," Thomas said, herding them back to the farm.

They went straight to the barn. Jordan and Robert were standing at the entrance. They must have read the bad news on everyone's faces, because they didn't ask any questions, just stood back, their hands in their pockets.

The big doors were partly open. Rosie stood in the doorway, pressing against the crack. Megan knew she was trying to get out to find her foal, but the opening wasn't wide enough for her. Only Sweetie had been able to slip through.

Thomas pressed his hand gently to the mare's shoulder to move her back from the door, and they all squeezed inside.

Rosie was sweating, agitated, trying to get out as if she knew that's where Sweetie had gone.

Tears filled Megan's eyes again. She couldn't stand seeing the mare wanting to follow her baby. How could she explain to her that he'd never be back?

Silently, they watched Thomas put a halter on the mare and lead her back to her stall, though she was balky and kept pulling away.

Thomas looked carefully at the stall door before leading Rosie in. He shot the bolt.

"The latch was open." He showed them. "It must have been closed, but not secured. The foal could have easily bumped it with his head until it jostled open."

Closed but not secured. The words rattled around in Megan's mind for a moment before taking hold. *Closed but not secured.*

Thomas fingered the metal latch carefully for a second.

"I don't want to pin anyone down here," he said, not unkindly. "The fact is that we all go in and out of these stalls every day. There are consequences for not checking the latch. The first rule on any farm: Check the gate, check the latch." He looked at each of them in turn.

Megan shriveled when his gaze fell on her. She had left the door open only yesterday. Did she do it again?

No. She was sure she'd locked it after giving Sweetie his afternoon grain. *I locked it, I checked it*, Megan insisted to herself.

Thomas went on. "As far as I can tell, Sweetie must have wandered out and stumbled trying to go down the hill. That sort of thing happens with foals, especially if the grass is wet and he was running." He spread his hands. "There's nothing we can do."

Outside, Megan could hear Dave start up the backhoe. She didn't have to be told that he was going to bury Sweetie.

Thomas left, and Isaac and Robert followed him out. Jordan put his arms around Megan. She started crying again, and he gave her a long, hard hug.

"I have to help Dave with the backhoe. I'll come find you when I'm done," he said as he left.

The barn was empty now. Good. She didn't want to talk. Megan leaned over the half door of the stall and stroked Rosie's damp nose over and over. *Your baby is dead*, she tried to communicate to the mare. *He's not coming back. He fell, and now he's gone.* Rosie's soft, intelligent eyes looked back at her. Megan thought maybe she understood.

Megan wanted to collapse on the barn floor and curl into a ball, but forced herself back outside. She was on the schedule to weed the garden today, her least favorite job.

Anna stood in the middle of the path.

"I didn't know you were still here."

"Are you kidding? Leave my friend in her time of need?" Anna entwined her arm with Megan's. Her skin felt cool and smooth, while Megan felt coated in sweat and grime from her run through the pasture. All she wanted was to take a shower and be alone.

"I have a headache," she said.

"Too bad!" Anna chirped. "I wish I had some Advil to give you."

Megan began plodding toward the garden.

"Don't you want some breakfast?" Anna kept up by her side.

Megan made a face. She couldn't think of anything she wanted less. "Let's just do the garden, okay? Then I want to take a shower and a nap."

"Well, that's understandable." Anna leaned over as they walked. "Sweetie's dead. He was, like, your best friend here, wasn't he? And so sad to die in such a violent way." She lowered her voice to a moist whisper. "Do you think it was breaking his neck that did it? Or if he'd just broken his legs, they'd have had to shoot him anyway, right? Like in the Kentucky Derby, remember, when they had to shoot that—"

"Stop!" Megan yelled. She felt a wave of anger at Anna's tone. "Just shut up about Sweetie! Why are you saying those things? I can hardly stand to think of him lying there, and you're going on like some disgusting ambulance chaser—" Fresh sobs drowned out her words.

"Soorrry," Anna drew the word out, widening her eyes. "I was just thinking out loud. Don't get all pissy." She didn't look fazed at Megan's outburst, which made Megan feel even more hurt.

In the garden, Robert was already bent over the carrots, busily pulling weeds, a tree-shaped sweat stain climbing up his back.

Megan inwardly groaned. She couldn't stand a repeat of last night's Anna-and-Robert Show. But Anna just waved to him and solicitously led Megan to a shaded corner near the pumpkins. "Let's weed here awhile where it's cooler." She started busily pulling strangleweed from the bases of the vines.

Megan just sat, feeling depressed and hot, while Anna worked her way from one end of the pumpkin patch to the other, stopping to whisper something to Robert at the end of the row. He nodded, and they both turned to Megan like concerned parents.

Megan resisted the urge to scream at Anna's worried face and, instead, ripped up a giant dandelion by the leaves.

Robert said something to Anna, then gave Megan a friendly wave and left the garden, heading back toward the farmhouse.

Anna had made a pile of the strangleweed and was working her way back toward Megan, this time pulling up violets. She paused, still on her knees, and dabbed at her forehead. "It's *so* humid, isn't it?" she said cheerfully.

Megan nodded.

Anna reached for a clump of nettles and yanked. "You know, I was thinking about yesterday," she said. "About how you left the stall open."

A wave of nausea broke over Megan.

"I mean, whoever did it this time basically killed Sweetie, right?" Anna's tone was conversational.

"I checked it." Megan's voice trembled. "I made sure I checked it *because* of yesterday."

"But you can't be one hundred percent sure, right?" Anna efficiently scraped the weeds together into one big pile, scooped them up, and walked toward the garden shed, her step crisp.

Megan rested her head on her knees. *Did you check it, Megan?* a voice asked in her head. *You* can't *be one hundred percent sure, right?*

For the first time, a worm of doubt squirmed into her mind. She pictured herself closing the stall door behind Sweetie's little form, then sliding the bolt to the right, then twisting it down. The twist down locked it.

In her mind's eye, she could see her hands making the motion. The picture was so clear, she could even see the hangnail on her finger.

But then, as Megan stared down into the dark hollow between her knees, the picture changed. Her hands closed the stall door and slid the bolt, but then they stopped. No twist.

Which is the right image? Megan pressed her hands to the sides of her head, willing herself to remember. She squeezed harder, as if to force the right memory into her mind.

Someone touched her shoulder. She started. It was Jordan.

He sat down beside her. "How're you holding up, Meg?"

She shook her head, knowing she was close to tears again. "I thought I was sure I latched the door. I thought I knew." Her voice was thick. "But now . . ." She groped for his hand. "What if it was me? What if I didn't slide the bolt all the way? What if he died because of me?" Her voice broke, and she swiped at the tears that flowed freely down her cheeks.

"Hey, now." Jordan drew her head to his chest and stroked her hair. "Hey. Thomas said it could have been any of us. You can't torture yourself like this. You'll go crazy."

"But he was suffering. . . ." Megan almost couldn't get the words out. She could hardly stand the thought of Sweetie alone and in pain at the bottom of that muddy hill. Wanting his mother. Her heart broke, and she buried fresh sobs in Jordan's shirt.

"Meg, stop." He lifted her chin with one finger. "You've got to stop."

His tone irritated her, and she lashed out at him. "Why should I stop? Am I not allowed to be sad?"

"No, of course you are." He patted her hand. "It's just . . . crying won't bring Sweetie back."

Anger boiled up in Megan, and she leapt to her feet. "I know that! Don't you think I know that? Maybe I'm crying because I miss him. Did that occur to you?" she blazed.

Jordan got to his feet too. "I know you miss him, okay? It's just . . ." He searched around for words. "I don't know, when I'm upset, I like to do something practical. Not just sit and cry."

"I can't believe you!" Megan knew she was shouting, but she couldn't stop herself. She wanted to lash out, to throw something. "Sweetie *died*, Jordan. He fucking *died*, and you're telling me to pick myself up and move on?"

"Well, yeah. Kind of." He met her gaze.

Megan dropped her hands to her sides. "Wow. Just . . . wow. I can't believe you'd be such a dick."

The word angered him. He folded his lips tightly. "That's really mature."

"I don't care!" Megan yelled. "I can be as immature as I want and cry all day. *You* don't get to decide how I feel!" She stomped through the pumpkins to the garden gate.

Then she saw Anna standing by the shed, a spade in her hand. She'd heard the whole fight, Megan could see that. But the look on Anna's face. Megan couldn't quite understand it at first. Then she realized—Anna was trying to hide her laughter.

CHAPTER 15

Anna saw Megan look at her and retreated back into the garden shed. Megan's gaze traveled from the black square of the doorway to Jordan's face, which was still cold with anger. She turned and ran.

Her thoughts chased her, temporarily driving her fight with Jordan from her mind. *Anna laughed. She was amused . . . because I was fighting with Jordan? But she said it was okay that Jordan and me were together. She made out with Robert!*

Megan slowed to a trot. The cabin was just ahead. She was so confused. She needed to lie down on her bed.

Megan pushed open the screen door. Though hot, the inside was blessedly dim. She felt like she could stand almost anything but the coppery glare of the sun.

Megan collapsed onto her rumpled bed. She lay there still, one arm crooked over her eyes, letting her thoughts slow until one by one, they clicked through her mind.

Anna had laughed at her fight with Jordan. That would mean

it made her happy. Why would that make her happy unless she wasn't really over Jordan? Had Anna been lying?

Megan sat up. She had a pit in her stomach. Her gaze traveled over to Anna's side of the room. Her bed was neatly made, the pillow plumped. So, she hadn't rushed out this morning like she said. On her bedside table, a few hair clips sat in a bowl next to a vase of daisies. Her trunk was closed. There was nothing else to see.

Megan's hands itched. Now that she had the thought in her head, she couldn't contain it, like a cancer that grew and grew. Slowly, she rose and knelt at Anna's trunk. She tugged at the lid.

Locked.

Megan sat back on her heels and stared at the trunk. It was black with dull brass fittings. She hadn't even realized that it had a lock, but it did. There was a small keyhole above the latch. Megan looked around the room. Her heart was beating fast now. She picked a long bobby pin out of the bowl by Anna's bed and bent one end down. She stuck it in the keyhole, rattled it around, pressing it alternately up, then down. Something moved inside the lock, and Megan took out the pin and tried the lid. It lifted easily.

She saw nothing inside but layers of neatly folded clothes, the same ones Anna'd been wearing since they arrived. She pulled out several pairs of sandals, tossed them on the bed. A paperback copy of *Hamlet*. Nothing.

Then, peeking out from a pair of jeans at the bottom of the trunk was a grass green crocheted bag. Megan recognized it. Anna had made it in eighth grade. Megan herself had crocheted a blue one with her.

Megan pulled it out and unbuttoned the closure. A square of gray fabric tipped out onto her palm. Megan stared at it for a second before recognizing it as the piece of Jordan's shirt that Anna had cut when they first arrived. The pearl-handled razor was stuffed into the bag too. Megan pulled it out. The case was slightly greasy and had a familiar odor she couldn't quite place. She unfolded the razor and sniffed the blade. It had been oiled recently—that was the smell. Megan reached into the bag and pulled out the last item, a piece of stiff paper.

It was a photograph, folded in half, and Megan stared at it in puzzlement for a long moment. Then she realized it was the picture Thomas had taken of the whole summer crew that first day. She and Jordan stood beside each other. Anna stood on her other side. But Anna's face had been cut out and was stuck crudely over Megan's. Megan held the photo loosely by the edges, as if it were poisoned. Her mind felt numb. Megan picked at the piece of tape on the picture until Anna's face peeled away.

Underneath, Megan's own face had been scraped from the photo. A blank white oval sat atop her shoulders. Anna's small face grinned up at Megan from where she'd dropped it.

Then the cabin door opened. Megan started. Anna stood in the doorway. She wore the same grin as in the photo.

"Came back to get my sunglasses." She strolled forward casually. Her eyes moved from the lock to the bobby pin lying on the floor to the items strewn on the bed. She raised her eyebrows. "I didn't know I'd find you breaking into my stuff."

Megan held up the photo. "What is this?" she whispered.

Her lips felt clumsy. Betrayal mixed with fear almost choked her.

Anna hesitated. She picked up the razor from the bed and the piece of Jordan's shirt. Then she shrugged.

"You might as well know." Her eyes glittered. "It's been fun, but it's time we talked." She sat down on the bed, opening and closing the razor casually in her hand.

Megan watched her. Her fear had subsided, and she felt curiously distant from herself, as if a cool observer of her own life.

Anna opened the razor. The metal was a silky gray. Meditatively, she ran her thumb over the blade. A deep cut appeared, white at first, then welling deep ruby red.

The blood dripped onto the gray blanket. There was quite a lot of it. It was a deep cut.

Anna looked at Megan from under her lashes. "I'm sure you know it was me who put the roaches in your bed." The blood was running down her hand now.

Megan thought of the squirming brown-green mass on her pillow. She stared at Anna, too shocked to move. The sight of the blood riveted her to the bed.

Anna looked slightly impatient. "Megan, come on. Don't be such an innocent little girl. It was me, it was me, it was me." Her voice rose with each intonation. She held the razor by the blade, then closed her hand around it and squeezed. The blood flowed from her clenched fist.

The fear was back, rising up strong in Megan's mouth. She darted a glance at the door. But Anna followed her gaze and rose sinuously, sauntering across the room to lean against the door with one knee drawn up. Her shirt pulled up a little, revealing her perfectly tanned stomach. The underside of her arm was smeared with blood. Blood puddled on the wool blanket where Anna had been sitting.

Anna gazed up at the ceiling. "And I was the one who killed your little colt." She reached down, tucking up her shirt, and drew the razor across her stomach in a short line just above her navel. The blood beaded. "I hit him with a stick until he ran down that hill. I knew he'd fall." She cut herself again, another straight line above the first cut. "He was scared." Another cut. "He tried to get away, but I smacked him hard and he ran right down that hill—"

"Stop," Megan whispered. Her mind roiled. Shakily, she rose from the bed, holding her hands out in a warding-off gesture. "Stop, you're sick. Stop."

Anna cut her stomach again.

"Stop!" Megan shrieked. "Oh my God, what's wrong with you, Anna? You're crazy!" She backed away from the bed.

The door. She had to get away, she had to get out the door. But Anna was standing in front of it.

Anna closed her eyes, leaning her head back. The cuts on her stomach were bleeding freely, the blood trickling down her belly, soaking the low waistband of her jeans.

Megan edged closer. She wasn't sure what she was going to do. Shove Anna to the side and run for help? Would Anna attack her? She had the razor. . . .

Anna opened her eyes. She saw Megan and smiled beatifically. "It's all your fault, you know."

Megan stopped.

"*All* your fault," Anna repeated, as sweet and calm as a spring-water pool. "If you weren't such a traitorous slut, none of this would have happened." She wandered back across the room and sat down on her bed, causing the cuts on her stomach to gape. She smiled up at Megan. "Ugly traitorous slut." Her voice caressed the words. She closed her eyes again, rocking her head slightly from side to side, then opened them, and leaning forward, reached into the drawer of her bedside table. She pulled out a bottle of nail polish.

The door was free now, but Megan watched, hypnotized, as Anna unscrewed the cap. She pulled out the brush and wiped it dry on the blanket beside her. With slow deliberation, she dipped the brush into a pool of her blood. She raised her knee and swiped the brush up and down her big toenail. Dip, swipe. Dip, swipe. Methodically, Anna worked her way across each toe.

Megan was frozen in horror, unable to take her eyes from Anna's hands.

Dip, swipe.

When she had finished the toenails on her right foot, Anna looked up again. Her eyes danced and sparkled. Her cheeks were delicately flushed. Megan thought she'd never seen Anna look so beautiful.

Anna knocked the bottle of polish to the floor. A pool of Sugar Daddy pink dripped onto the rough floorboards. Anna dipped her brush into the pool of blood on the blanket, but finding it congealed, simply slashed her belly again. The blood flowed red, and she began to paint her left toenails.

"I want Jordan." Anna said it offhandedly, as if ordering a burger.

Megan couldn't have responded even if she'd wanted to. Her mouth had gone dry.

Anna finished with her toes. She stretched her feet out, admiring her work, then pulled back the covers and climbed into bed, smearing the sheets with blood, as she lay on her side. She pulled the blankets up over her shoulders, then looked at Megan. Anna's black hair spread out on the pillow. She yawned like a cat, showing pearly white teeth and a delicate pink tongue.

"I'll make it very simple for you. Break up with Jordan. Tell him you don't love him. I saw you guys fighting this afternoon. It shouldn't be hard."

She closed her eyes for a long moment, and Megan wondered if she'd passed out from blood loss or gone to sleep.

Then she said slowly, "Do it today. And make it good. He'd better believe you. If he doesn't . . . or if you breathe one tiny word about this to Thomas"—her jaws cracked in another yawn—"well . . . you know, I can't guarantee what will happen next."

Anna pulled the razor out from under the covers and placed it on her pillow. Her sleepy eyes opened a fraction of an inch, and Megan saw her smile at it, like you'd smile at the face of a lover. Then Anna's eyes closed and she fell asleep.

CHAPTER 16

"He's out with the pigs," Anna whispered softly in Megan's ear.
They walked quickly along the path. Megan nodded and swallowed. All around them, everything seemed normal. Dave chugged by on the tractor and raised his hand to them. They passed Isaac and Robert forking dirty bedding onto the manure pile by the barn. Sarah was bent over in the garden, pulling carrots. But Megan felt as if an icy scrim had fallen between her and the rest of the world. Only she and Anna knew what was really happening.

Megan thought of that famous kidnapping case where a robber walked a woman into a bank in broad daylight and made her withdraw money for him. There'd been lots of people around, but no one knew anything was wrong until she managed to pass the teller a note. But the robber found out and he killed her.

Megan glanced at Anna, who walked half a step behind her. She'd washed most of the blood off her face and arms. Her ears were still crusted with some dark red flakes. Anna stepped lightly, eagerly, and occasionally gave Megan's arm a confiding little squeeze with her bandaged hand. Her fingers were cold.

Megan could see Jordan spreading a bale of straw in the pigs' bed corner, his back to the road. Anna melted behind a nearby stand of blackberry brambles just as he turned around. He smiled when he saw Megan and waved, coming toward her. She knew he was going to apologize for the fight. She readied herself. *Make it good.*

"We have to talk." Her words were harsh and abrupt.

The smile dropped from his lips. "Meg, if this is about before—"

"Not here." She could hardly believe the cold composure in her own voice. Out of the corner of her eye, she saw the brambles rustle. "Later, okay? It's important. The old barn, tonight. Ten o'clock." Anna had insisted that be their meeting place.

He reached for her. "Megan, what's going on? Tell me now." He touched her forearm, but she recoiled. The brambles rustled again.

"No. Later." She spun around, not daring to look back but feeling his eyes on her as she retreated down the road.

"Megan."

Anna shook her shoulder roughly, and Megan's eyes flew open. Anna's face hovered above her own. Black eyeliner ringed both her eyes, so that they appeared to be glittering from the bottom of two holes. Her orange lipstick was crooked and gleamed in the dim lantern light.

Anna trailed a finger down the side of Megan's cheek, then playfully squeezed her chin. "It's time."

The cool air caressed Megan as they stepped out into the night. The farm lay sleeping around them. The sheep were snuggled against each other as they made their way past the pasture fence and around to the old barn at the back.

Megan's flashlight bounced across the rotted siding to the gaping mouth of the doorway. She couldn't tell if Jordan was already inside or not. Carefully, she pressed her hand against her pocket to stifle any telltale rustles. She'd managed to sequester herself in the bathroom before dinner and scribble a quick note.

> Everything I'm saying is a lie. Anna is forcing me to break up with you so she can have you for herself. I'm scared. Something's wrong with her—and she has a razor. Meet me tonight at the bonfire place in the woods. Three o'clock. Don't tell anyone! Please—we have to figure out what to do. I love you. M.

Anna stood behind her, so close, Megan could hear her breath—light, quick. There was a soft, metallic *zing!*

"Don't try to run away," Anna said. "I wouldn't recommend it." Megan felt the back of her shirt lift and something cold and sharp pressed into her skin below her shoulder blades. Megan opened her mouth but couldn't scream. She couldn't run. She was frozen in fear.

Anna drew the razor down in a quick diagonal line almost to Megan's waist. The pain trailed behind the pressure of the blade in a thin burning line. Another diagonal, top to bottom. Megan could feel droplets of wetness she knew was blood. Then Anna drew a short straight line connecting the two. The letter *A*. Carved on her back.

Anna dropped Megan's shirt and leaned next to her ear. "Showtime, Meg." Then she slipped into the darkness.

Megan faced the doorway and shined her flashlight into its maw. The feeble beam barely pierced the darkness. She stepped onto the rotting boards. Suddenly she wondered if this was a trap. *Is Anna going to do something to Jordan?* Megan stifled a sob and played her flashlight quickly over the old machinery, the fallen stall dividers. The light picked out a figure standing in the middle of the floor. She opened her mouth to scream until she realized it was Jordan.

He wore a gray sweatshirt, his hands buried in the front pocket, his face set in angry lines. Megan wanted to run to him and bury her head in his chest, but the pain in her back reminded her of what she had to do.

"Hi," she said. The word sounded silly in this setting.

He didn't answer for a minute, just looked at her. "So you dragged me all the way out here just to break up with me?" His voice was harsh. "Great, Meg. This is just great." He fell silent again.

Do it. Scanning the small windows, she wondered where Anna was. They were all black.

"Jordan, it's over." Megan carefully spoke the words Anna had told her to say. "I never thought you could be such a jerk like you were this afternoon." She felt sick at the look on his face. The real words she wanted to say crowded her mouth. *I love you. This is all a lie.* Over his shoulder, a moonlike white face appeared at one of the windows. Anna was watching.

Jordan slowly shook his head. "I don't understand. Please, can we talk about this?"

"No." Megan winced at the brutality of the words. "I'm leaving the farm anyway. Thomas is kicking me out." That was a lie, of course, but Anna had insisted.

"What? Are you serious? Because of the latch?"

"And other things . . ." Megan swallowed. She forced herself to go on. "He caught me with Robert."

"Caught you with Robert?"

Megan watched the meaning dawn on him. Then Jordan stepped forward and grasped her shoulders.

Now. This is the time. Megan moved one step closer and as quickly as she could wormed the note out of her shorts and stuffed it into his sweatshirt pocket. She was almost positive Jordan's body had blocked any view of the maneuver.

Jordan released her and stepped back. He looked like he was going to punch something. "No. You wouldn't. I thought I knew you better than that."

Megan stared up at him. *You do!* she tried to tell him with her eyes.

He turned his back. "I think you'd better leave."

Anna was nowhere to be seen by the time Megan got outside. With the bloody *A* on her back still burning with every step, Megan turned back toward the cabin.

CHAPTER 17

Anna was tucked into bed by the time Megan got back to the cabin. She looked like an angel with her hair in two neat braids and the white sheet folded neatly under her arms. She'd washed the makeup from her face, and her freshly scrubbed skin glowed against the pillow.

She smiled dreamily as Megan came in. "Meg, that was brilliant. Just brilliant."

Megan started taking off her clothes. Her fear had dissipated, leaving her oddly calm. The cuts on her back no longer stung. In the back of her mind, she wondered if she should wash them, but instead she pulled on a T-shirt and sweatpants and climbed into bed.

"Thanks," she said. It was the first thing she'd said to Anna all evening. Her voice even sounded normal. Jordan knew by now. She wasn't alone in this anymore.

Megan resisted turning her face to the wall, in case Anna

came at her with the razor. But there was no need. Anna seemed calmed by the scene in the barn, and within only a few minutes, her breathing had slowed to a regular rhythm. She was asleep.

Megan lay in the dark, staring at the gray square of the door, wondering where Anna had stashed the razor. The minutes dragged past. Anna murmured something indistinct and rolled over in bed. An owl called his odd chattering hoot out in a nearby tree. Moths and bugs tinged against the metal screen door.

At two thirty, Megan carefully slid from the bed and pulled on her jeans. She stuck her feet into her unlaced sneakers. Anna was a long lump under the covers across the room. Megan briefly imagined Anna awakening, her eyes glittering over the top of the sheet. Her heart thudded. Megan eased the screen door open. It creaked. She froze. But there was no movement from the bed.

Megan broke into a run as soon as her feet touched the bare dirt of the path. She didn't look back. In her mind's eye, Anna stood behind her on the porch, her long hair flying wild, clutching the razor like a younger Bertha Rochester.

Megan stopped to tie her sneakers, then ran through the open fields bright with moonlight toward the woods. As she entered the trees, she realized she'd forgotten her flashlight. Briefly, she panicked at the darkness, but the thought of Jordan waiting spurred her on.

The path became rougher as it wound up the steep hill toward the bonfire site. Megan slowed, her eyes trained on the ground to keep from stumbling. She was almost to the first switchback. On her left, the ravine gaped like an open mouth.

"Meg!" Jordan stood on the path several yards above her. She sighed with relief. He ran toward her, catching her by the hand.

"Here, down here." He pulled her off the path, down the steep slope.

"Is this safe?" Megan gasped. She realized the irony of the question as soon as it was out of her mouth and laughed shakily.

"It's okay, there's a creek at the bottom." He had a flashlight and held her elbow to guide her. "Watch the rocks."

They inched down the slope sideways like crabs, arms out for balance. As they went lower, Megan's eyes adjusted, and she saw the meandering creek bed strewn with rocks, scattered about like pebbles on a giant's playground.

They stumbled to the bottom, then Jordan took Megan's face in both hands. His eyes searched hers. He pulled her close. Megan let out a huge shuddering sigh as she pressed into him and felt his arms wrapped around her tightly. It hurt her cuts, but she didn't care. Tears leaked out from beneath her eyelids.

Jordan pulled back and gazed down at her. "Robert's so not your type." He grinned.

Megan let out a half laugh, half sob. "How can you joke about this?"

"What's the alternative?" he asked, his voice soft. He brushed her hair back from her face, then leaned down and kissed her, long and deep. She pressed up against him, her arms around his neck. His fingers rubbed her shoulders, then slid down to her waist. She inhaled sharply.

"What is it?" Jordan asked.

Megan shook her head. "Nothing. It's just . . . she cut me earlier with the razor. Before I went into the barn. On my back."

She turned and lifted her shirt, then heard him gasp. "Jesus." Megan faced him.

"Look, we'll figure this out," he said. "We'll do it together." He rested his forehead against hers, and they stood like that for a long moment.

Relief flooded Megan. She felt exhausted and nervous with energy at the same time.

Then she heard a clattering. A huge rock bounced down the ravine toward them, tearing up bushes as it fell. A shadow flitted along the top edge of the ravine.

"Jordan!" Megan screamed.

He jumped aside, pulling her along with him, just as the rock rolled over the very spot they'd been standing.

"Someone's up there," Megan gasped. "Anna! She must have followed me here."

Jordan looked around and switched off his flashlight. "Okay, we'll go up the creek bed. It's narrower. She won't be able to see us in the dark."

They ran holding hands, stumbling on the rocks, trying not to fall. Megan scanned the top of the ridge constantly. Jordan stopped after a minute and began climbing up the steep slope.

"What are you doing?" Megan whispered frantically. "She's up there! She knows I lied to her. She's capable of anything now."

"I know," Jordan said. "There's no time to go to Thomas." He scrabbled over a boulder, his sweaty shirt clinging to his back. Megan's sneakers slipped and slid in the loose dirt as they climbed. "We have to get to her first. She could beat us to the farmhouse and do something awful."

They bellied over the top of the ravine and scrambled to their feet. Megan looked around. All she could see in the silver light were tree trunks and the thick layer of dead leaves underfoot. Then a sharp crack came from the left as a branch broke.

Jordan took off running toward the noise. "Come on!" he said.

Megan followed, the adrenaline pumping through her veins. Her breath whistled in her throat.

They found Anna struggling to roll another boulder closer to the ravine, thinking they were still down there. She looked up as they approached, and Megan caught her breath.

She'd been cutting herself again—Megan could see that right away. The belly of her torn gray T-shirt was stained with fresh blood. But this time, she'd painted her face with it. Dried blood was slashed in a clown's smile across her mouth, and she'd smeared it on her cheeks like blush, over her eyes like eye shadow. She must have done it after she'd found Megan gone.

"Anna," Jordan breathed, slowing to a halt, clearly shocked by the sight of her face. Megan stopped a few feet behind him. She couldn't tell if Anna noticed her or not, she was so focused on Jordan.

"Anna, we know you pushed that rock. It almost killed us," Jordan said. He moved a few steps to the right. Megan could tell he was looking to see if she had the razor.

Anna's stance suddenly changed. Her body relaxed, and she dropped her head bashfully. She swayed toward Jordan.

Megan backed up until she was in the deep shadow of a nearby tree.

"Jordan, please help me," Anna said in a sexy voice. "You're the only one who can help me." She looped her arms around his neck and laid her head on his shoulder. "I'm sick, baby. I need help."

Jordan shuddered, Megan guessed at the smell of the blood. He tried to peel her off of him. "Anna, you do. You do need help." He spoke gently. "I'm going to help you, okay?"

"Yes." Anna was panting now. "Help me." She pressed herself against him, her head tilted up, trying to kiss him. "Jordan, I love you."

"Stop, okay?" Jordan pried her arms from around his neck, lifting his face away from her searching lips. "We'll take you to Thomas. He'll help us."

Anna didn't seem to hear him. "Jordan," she breathed. She leaned toward him and licked his neck. "You don't need that bitch. You need me. She's frigid. I can do anything for you. . . ." Her voice trailed off into a whisper. She tried to slide her hands down the waist of his jeans.

"Anna!" Jordan's voice rose. He pushed her away, held her by her bandaged hands. "Listen to me. You're delusional. I don't love you. I'm with Megan, do you hear me? I love her. That's the truth—not whatever story you're making up in your head."

Anna stared at him, her eyes huge. She started trembling, then shaking, until her whole body was swaying with the tremors. Still staring right into Jordan's face, she opened her mouth and screamed, an eerie, keening wail. Again and again she screamed. It was a horrible sound. Megan cowered against the tree trunk and covered her ears.

Anna broke from Jordan's grasp and fell to the ground, her hands pulling at her head. She screamed as she ripped out clumps of her hair. Blood trickled down her face. She screamed again, baying at the sky. Her fingers went to her eyes.

In a flash, Megan remembered their tenth-grade English project: *King Lear*'s famous scene of the blinding of Gloucester. She ran forward. "Anna, stop, stop!" she sobbed. She fell to her knees in front of her friend and seized her wrists. "Please!"

At Megan's touch, Anna turned her head in one short, swift movement, like a lizard. She studied Megan's face. Then she rose and bared her teeth. Her lips were shredded and bleeding where she'd bitten them. She growled deep in her throat. Anna broke Megan's grasp, and her hand went to her back pocket. The metal of the razor blade flashed.

"Stop!" Megan gasped. She raised her hands to protect her face and caught the slash of the blade on the back of one hand.

"Megan!" Jordan shouted. He ran forward, hitting Anna with his own body. Anna fell to the ground. The razor flew from her hand, landing somewhere in the darkness.

Anna's whole body went still. Her eyes were vacant, and her hands lay limply beside her on the ground as if detached from the rest of her body. She began rocking back and forth. Back and forth. Megan and Jordan backed away.

"Anna?" Megan whispered tentatively.

She didn't answer. She just kept rocking rhythmically, staring off somewhere into the trees.

"Come on," Jordan said quietly to Megan.

They ran.

The eastern sky held a tinge of gray when they reached the farmhouse. Megan ran up the steps with Jordan close behind. Her lungs were burning, her hand still bleeding.

"Thomas!" she yelled, struggling with the kitchen door. "Thomas!" Inside, the house was still asleep.

"Thomas!" Jordan shouted up the stairs.

A moment later, the hall light went on and Thomas appeared at the top of the stairs, his hair disheveled. "What? What is it?" He hurried down the steps. "The animals? What?"

"No." Megan tried to catch her breath. "It's Anna. Something's really wrong with her. She tried to kill us." As fast as she could, she poured out the story as Jordan paced anxiously by her side. "We have to stop her," Megan said. "She could do anything."

Thomas's forehead wrinkled. "Megan," he said slowly, "are you sure about this? These are serious accusations. This isn't some kind of misunderstanding? . . ." He looked at her bleeding hand. "Did you two have a fight?"

Megan almost screamed with impatience. "No, please, Thomas! We have to do something fast. You have to believe me, she isn't—"

Jordan stopped her with an upraised hand. "What's that?"

Everyone froze, listening. There was a crackling on the kitchen porch. Thomas sniffed. "Smoke." His eyes went wide. "Linda!" He turned and ran toward the stairs. Jordan ran behind him.

"Get outside!" Jordan shouted to Megan. Anna was laughing hysterically outside the window. Wisps of smoke curled under the door and around the window frame. The shrill of a smoke detector pierced the room. The crackling grew louder. Flames leapt up outside the window.

Megan ran for the door and grabbed the knob, then let go with a gasp. The metal was scorching hot. She grabbed a dishtowel from the counter and twisted the knob. It wouldn't open. She pushed with all her might, but something was blocking it. Anna had shoved something against it. They were trapped, and the house was rapidly filling with smoke.

"Anna!" Megan screamed. She pounded on the door, coughing, her eyes burning. Then she felt heat at her back and turned. The fire was at the front of the house now—she could see it in the living room. The kitchen door was the only way out.

"Get out of the way!" Jordan shouted from behind her. Thomas stood beside him, holding Linda in his arms. Jordan threw his whole weight against the door. It shuddered in its frame.

"Help him, Thomas!" Linda cried. She coughed violently. The room was hot now.

Megan had a sudden thought. "Dave and Sarah!" she cried.

"Gone for the night!" Thomas shouted back.

Megan's lungs were burning. Each breath was harder to draw than the last. She wondered how it would feel to suffocate. Anna was screaming with laughter outside.

Thomas sat Linda in a chair, and then together, he and Jordan slammed their shoulders at the door. Again. Again. How could it resist those tremendous blows? *They have to get it open—Linda can never get out a window*, Megan thought frantically.

Finally, the door shuddered. The wood split, and with a crash, the door gave, spilling them out onto the burning porch. Gasping, Jordan grabbed Megan and pushed her to safety. The burning boards gave way beneath her feet. Megan threw herself forward, tumbling down the steps, and on her elbows, pulled herself across the grass, away from the flames, just as Thomas shoved Linda to the ground beside her.

Megan lifted her head as Anna danced before them manically, a can of kerosene in her hand. Anna lifted the can and poured it over her head in a deadly shower.

Anna flicked her lighter. Flames exploded from her hair and clothes.

"No!" Megan screamed.

Jordan threw himself forward, knocking Anna to the ground and smothering the flames with his body.

The fire roared with massive orange power, climbing to the second story. Flames shot out the bedroom windows, and a shower of glass and ash rained down on the lawn.

"Help us, someone," Megan moaned. Thomas knelt on the lawn, his head in his hands, and Anna sobbed in defeat as the house was slowly consumed.

EPILOGUE

One Year Later

"So, I'm going to see you in two weeks." Jordan hugged Megan tightly as they leaned against the sun-warmed metal of his Wrangler, which was parked in her driveway. "You're not allowed to be sad. Then I'll be sad, and I still have to drive three hours back to school."

"I know." Megan sighed. Jordan was at Ohio State, like he'd planned. It wasn't too bad in terms of a long-distance relationship. She planted one last kiss on his lips, lingering as long as she dared. Her mother was probably watching from the living room window.

Jordan held her close for another moment, then kissed her quickly and climbed into the car. "I love you," he said, leaning out the window. The sun gleamed on his red-gold hair.

"I love you, too." Megan waved as he backed down the driveway and his car turned the corner. She sighed, already feeling the sharp stab of his absence. Still, it *was* only two weeks.

Smiling a little to herself, Megan wandered back to the house.

"Well, that's it. I'm officially bereft for the next fourteen days," she called into the dim foyer.

Her mother appeared in the doorway of the dining room, her reading glasses pushed up onto her forehead. Her brow was furrowed.

"It's okay, Mom." Megan went over to her, a little surprised. "I was just kidding. I mean, I *am* sad, but—"

Her mother cut her off. "Meg, come sit down, honey. I have to talk to you about something."

Megan sank into a chair, her hands suddenly cold. The last time her mother looked that way was four years ago, when her cousin Lanie had died.

Her mother took her glasses off and put them on again. She seemed to be having trouble getting started. "You know I've kept in touch with Anna's mother this year—"

"I don't want to talk about that," Megan said flatly, just like she always did whenever her parents brought up Anna.

Her mother put her hand on Megan's knee. "Anna's been released from Greenbriar."

Megan tensed.

"She's made a lot of progress, Janine said. And she's been released to a halfway house, where she'll be closely supervised." Her mother squeezed Megan's hand between her own. "Really, Janine said she's like a different person. She almost didn't recognize her at the last visit. And anyway, it's not like you'll be seeing her. She's still near the Greenbriar campus, in Michigan."

Megan nodded. She took a deep breath and blew it out. "Right. I just want to put it all behind me." She slipped her hand from her mother's clasp and stood up.

"Of course you do," her mother said, standing and heading toward the kitchen. "I think that's just the right attitude."

"I'm going to take a shower before dinner," Megan called as she mounted the stairs to her room. She and Jordan had taken a long bike ride that afternoon, and she was feeling a little sweaty.

"Okay." The blender started up in the kitchen. Her mother raised her voice over the noise. "You got some mail. I put it on your desk."

In her room, Megan riffled through a batch of colorful college circulars. There was also a note from her grandmother, and at the bottom of the stack, a plain white envelope, with no return address. She flipped it over and ripped it open. A small square of gray fabric fluttered to the floor. Megan jumped back as if it were alive. With her heart pounding, Megan pulled an index card from the envelope. Three words were scribbled on one side.

See you soon.

ACKNOWLEDGMENTS

I'd like to thank my agent, Michael Bourret, for his unflagging support, and my editor, Annette Pollert. She manages to combine a sharp eye with endless patience. Thanks are also due to Emilia Rhodes, who guided this book through the very first stages. I would also like to express my appreciation for my husband, Aaron, who never doubts me, even when I doubt myself.

Some secrets are meant
to stay buried. . . .

DON'T MISS
EMMA CARLSON BERNE'S

STILL WATERS

The back door slapped flatly behind them as Hannah followed Colin back into the house. "I'll grab the bags from the car," he said over his shoulder, his step brisk and confident again. Hannah imagined his figure disturbing the thick, still air of the house, like a rippling eddy in a sluggish stream.

"Okay."

His footsteps descended the porch stairs. Hannah stood still in the center of the floor, feeling a thin layer of grit in the bottom of her sneakers, the frayed laces pressing on her instep. The room was perfectly silent except for a fly buzzing and bumping against the window. It must have come in with them. Outside, Colin slammed the car door. But even that sound was muffled in the heavy air that shrouded the room.

Hannah suddenly felt the distance around them, the miles of woods separating them from the nearest house, from even one road. Her breath hitched and a wave of claustrophobia tightened around her throat. The rough gray walls of the room seemed to rise around her, enclosing her in a high box. What were they doing here? What had she done? Running away like this—lying.

Quickly she moved to the near window and, twisting the stiff latch, shoved the splintery frame upward with all her strength. It resisted, and then gave with a groan. Hannah pressed her face against the rusty screen, inhaling the rich mud and grass odor that wafted in along with the rushing noise of the wind in the pine trees. The silence became more ordinary and the tightness in her throat slowly loosened.

Hannah turned, blowing out her lips in a long exhale. *Okay, get a grip. It's all going to be okay—Colin seems fine now. And the place is nice, actually.* She examined the room more closely. The wide gray board walls were unpainted and darkened with age. Overhead, the ceiling arched, crisscrossed with exposed rafters. On each outside wall, wide windows stretched, facing the lake, so that the water seemed like it was going to lap right up to the edge of the floorboards. Who cared if it was a little strange? *Hannah, you're here, alone with your boyfriend for the first time, really alone, at Pine House, and nothing to do but just lie around, eat, swim, talk.*

Swiftly, before she thought too much about what she was doing, she crossed to the sofa, where *Middlemarch* sat open beside the stained coffee cup. In one motion, she picked up the book, slamming it shut, and shoved it under the couch. Anything to get rid of it fast. She grabbed the coffee cup and carried it through to the kitchen, where she dropped it into the sink. Then, back in the living room, she plumped the couch cushions, choking a little on the dust, and smoothed them with both hands.

She stood back and surveyed her work. *You'd never know anyone had ever been there,* she thought just as the outside door slammed. This was *her* house now—hers and Colin's. Whatever had gone on here before was over.

She looked up as Colin came into the room with the duffel bags over each shoulder. Sweat beaded his forehead. "Hot out." He looked around. "There's a nice breeze in here though."

Hannah smiled with satisfaction. "Where do you want to sleep?" The words sounded ordinary but she felt a shiver go through her as she followed Colin's broad back down the hallway toward the bedrooms. A little giggle of anticipation escaped her like a bubble, and Colin turned around, smiling. His eyes gleamed in the shadowy darkness.

"What?" His voice was low and teasing, as if he'd already guessed what she was thinking.

"Nothing." His face was very close to hers.

"Nothing," he teased, imitating her. He grabbed her around the waist with the suddenness of a snake strike. She giggled again, and he stopped the laugh by pressing his mouth to hers. Hannah leaned into the kiss. His arm circled her waist, pulling her in closely, and Hannah felt her heart quicken. His lips were firm and insistent. He pressed her against him, and she felt her head fall back. A doorknob was digging into her back. Feeling behind her, she twisted the smooth china knob. The door swung open, and they almost fell into the room beyond.

It was the room with the big bed. Hannah, eyes mostly closed, let Colin press her backward onto the mattress. She felt him leaning over her. Smiling, she stretched her arms over her head, waiting for him to clasp her hands and kiss her again. But his body grew still.

Hannah opened her eyes. Colin was leaning over her, but his eyes were fixed on the small window opposite the bed.

Hannah craned her neck back, but all she could see out the window were trees and gray sky. "Colin?" she murmured.

He looked down at her as if surprised to see her there. "Hmm?"

"Are you okay?" she asked carefully.

He shook his head a little and blinked. "Of course." But he rolled over to one side.

Hannah raised herself up on an elbow and looked around. There wasn't much to see. Books stacked beside the bed: some Jane Austen and a dictionary. A closed closet door. The white bedspread. That was all.

"Was this your parents' room?" she asked.

Colin shook his head. "I don't know. I guess so. I already told you like six hundred times, Han, I don't remember this place. Okay?"

Hannah sighed. "Sorry. I'm just curious, and I don't have anyone else to ask."

"Okay, let's forget it." Colin smiled his easy grin. "You're so gorgeous on that white quilt. Hang on." He climbed off the bed and disappeared down the hall for a moment, returning with his camera in his hand.

"Okay, let's see it," he said, his camera already at his eye. Hannah grinned and scooted backward on the bed until she was half propped against the pillows. She struck a pose, arms behind her head, hips twisted to the side.

"Nice." Colin snapped a few shots. "Very Hollywood bombshell."

Hannah snorted and flipped onto her stomach. "All us bombshells wear jeans and T-shirts with"—she looked down at the words on her shirt—"Reider High Mathlympics on them." She sucked in her cheeks and aimed a sultry look at the camera.

Colin zoomed in, the camera clicking in an insectile manner.

"Hey, not too close!" Hannah protested, holding her hands up in front of her face.

"What do you mean 'not too close'? Like this?" Colin put a knee up on the bed and leaned over. Hannah giggled a little as he advanced closer, still holding the camera. He clicked off another shot and moved closer. She pressed herself back against the pillows and reached for him.

Colin shoved the camera to one side and bent over her. She closed her eyes, relishing the hot, insistent pressure of his lips on hers. Before Colin, she didn't even know what a kiss was. Howard Mortenson freshman year didn't count. Kissing him was like having someone toilet plunge her mouth. And after that, no one . . . until Colin.

Too soon, Colin drew his head back. He stretched out on his side next to her, propping his head up with his hand. His blue eyes were soft and sparkling. The sun must have come out because a dapple of sunlight played on the wall behind him. "Are you happy we came up here?" he asked.

She nodded, rolling a little closer to him. "Yeah. I can't believe we made it, but I'm really happy." She burrowed her face into the hard muscles of his chest. She could hear his heart beating slow, strong thuds. Her muscles felt limp, as if her body were filled with honey. She gazed into Colin's face, lazily stroking the side of his stubbly cheek with the tips of her fingers, smiling. This felt good. It felt right, finally, after all the angst from earlier.

Colin moved an inch closer. "Han . . ." His breath blew softly against her cheek. "I . . ."

She felt herself tighten up. No. Not yet. It was too soon. She wasn't ready right now. She rolled away from Colin and slid off the bed. He sighed and flopped back on the pillows, staring up at the ceiling.

Hannah stood at the edge of the bed, trying to gauge his level of frustration, chewing her lip. A little moment of silence stretched out—familiar silence. This was the silence they'd been inhabiting since he first spoke those three words graduation night. "You want to get something to eat?" she offered after a long moment. She tried a little smile.

"Sure." He sighed and shoved himself off the bed.

Just a little more time. That was all she needed, she told herself as she followed Colin down the hallway.

ABOUT THE AUTHOR

Emma Carlson Berne lives in Cincinnati, Ohio, with her husband, Aaron, and their sons, Henry and Leo. She is also the author of *Still Waters* and *Hard to Get*.

"Don't even *think* of leaving. . . .
I will find you," he whispered.
"Guaranteed."

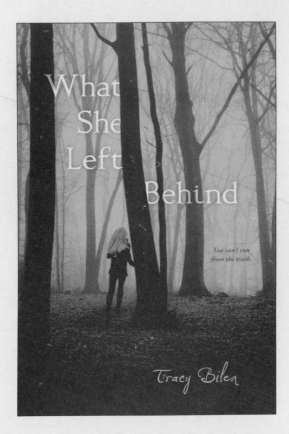

A chilling novel from

Tracy Bilen

THREE HEARTBREAKING AND GUT-WRENCHING STORIES ABOUT FRIENDSHIP, LOVE, AND LOSS

Lauren Strasnick

FALL IN LOVE…IF YOU DARE.

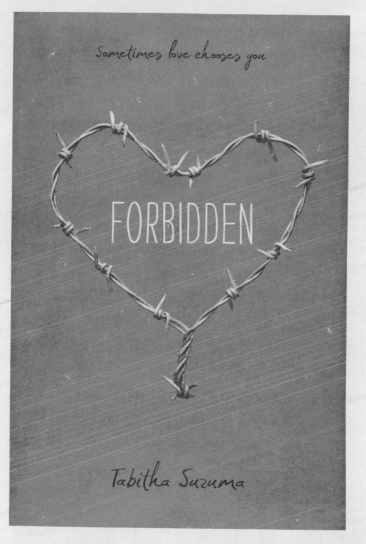

Sometimes love chooses you.

FORBIDDEN

Tabitha Suzuma

Need a distraction?

Lauren Strasnick

Arlaina Tibensky

Amy Reed

Christine Johnson

Deb Caletti

Lisa Schroeder

Eileen Cook

Charity Tahmaseb & Darcy Vance

Go Ahead, Ask Me.
Nico Medina & Billy Merrell

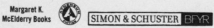

SiMON TEEN

Simon & Schuster's **Simon Teen**
e-newsletter delivers current updates on
the hottest titles, exciting sweepstakes, and
exclusive content from your favorite authors.

Visit **TEEN.SimonandSchuster.com** to
sign up, post your thoughts, and find out what
every avid reader is talking about!